TOO

Books in
The Jennifer Grey Mystery Series

TOO LATE TO TELL

A
Jennifer Grey
Mystery

Jerry B. Jenkins

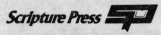

AMERSHAM-ON-THE-HILL, BUCKS HP6 6JQ
ENGLAND

Production and Printing in England for
SCRIPTURE PRESS FOUNDATION (UK) LTD
Raans Road, Amersham-on-the-Hill, Bucks HP6 6JQ by
Nuprint Ltd, 30b Station Road, Harpenden, Herts AL5 4SE.

1 As much as Jennifer Grey disliked Bobby Block, his mysterious note intrigued her. He had always been a young man of complex problems, one she had never been able to make out. Clearly, he had always envied her, and after only a brief period of conniving, he showed his true colours and tried opennly to destroy her. But Jennifer had survived.

Bobby had been a hulking, earnest, dark-haired student from Northwestern University's Medill School of Journalism when they had met. He was already in place as a special assistant to the police reporter when Jennifer was hand-picked by *Chicago Day* City Editor Leo Stanton to take over the police beat.

'You can dump Block, or you can teach him,' Stanton said in his usual blunt fifty-seven-year-old way. 'Your choice.'

'He could probably teach *me*,' Jennifer had

said, not kidding. 'I'll keep him for now, at least until I learn the ropes.'

Stanton had shrugged. 'He's OK, a little cocky. Lots of potential. We'll find a spot for him either way. I just don't want you to feel saddled. You've got the budget for part-time help, but you can hire your own if you wish.'

Jennifer hadn't wished. At least not at first. There had been many times since then that she would have given anything to have taken Leo up on his offer.

Bobby had been fine the first few days — telling Jennifer where everything was, introducing her to the key contacts in all the precincts. But she sensed something behind his superficial self-deprecating comments. It wasn't long before she realized that he was working against her.

Bobby Block may have doubted his own worth or ability, but his insecurities surfaced in quiet insubordination. At first, he had simply seemed eager to be in on everything and get his share of good by-lined stories.

But soon Bobby was thwarting Jennifer at every turn, withholding crucial information, leaking her best tips to the competition, and putting her in a bad light before Leo. Bobby wasn't openly hostile until he had got her into serious trouble; only then did it hit her that he had been the source of her problems.

In the middle of her coverage of an Internal Affairs Division (IAD) dragnet, Bobby chose to reveal Jennifer's relationship with Police Officer James Purcell, one of the charged officers. Until

Purcell was cleared, Jennifer had lost her job — which, of course, had been Bobby's intention.

Months later, when Jennifer graduated to a front-page column, Bobby was so incensed that he took to snooping around her stories, trying to scoop her. That cost him *his* job, and within hours he was snapped up by the *Tribune,* from which he had waged a smear campaign against Jennifer. He even tried to implicate her in a murder that she and Jim Purcell eventually solved.

That cooled Bobby's jets for a while, and except for an occasional veiled barb at Jennifer, Bobby had settled into his role as police reporter at the *Tribune.* He had graduated with honours, alienated classmates and profs, annoyed his superiors and co-workers, and raised the hackles of the police officers he needed as sources. Yet still he flourished.

His secret was good writing laced with sarcasm and satire. The readers loved it. But Bobby had a growing list of professional enemies who soon realized that little he had ever said about Jennifer Grey had been true.

Jennifer, however, had been left with a nagging conscience over her failure to ever get next to Bobby — to find out what it was that made him so obnoxious, so committed to making waves, so unhappy unless he was fighting. She felt she and Jim had something to offer Bobby. But she realized she had been naïve to think he would listen.

Twice she had called to make appointments with him, hoping to bury the hatchet, to just chat, to grab a bite at Berghoffs. Neither time did

Bobby even return her call. She had settled on what she would say, how she would begin. It wouldn't be that difficult, because she had grown to appreciate certain aspects of his writing.

She knew he was a better pure writer than she was, with less warmth and feeling and people-orientation perhaps, but with a certain concise purity nonetheless. And he had become a careful researcher. That surprised her. More than a few times she had recognized in his stories much careful homework and documentation of facts.

That was something she had tried to teach him over and over again, yet he had been content to skate over it, to guess, to assume. Maybe now that he was on his own at one of the top papers in the country, he felt forced to do it right. Or maybe someone was doing it for him.

Regardless, his writing had improved. She wanted to tell him that. But for a long time, Bobby pretended she didn't exist. She decided a cold war was better than his all-out efforts to ruin her had been in the past. Jennifer wished he would at least respond somehow, even if to say no to her invitation to lunch.

And then on Wednesday, his note had come. It read simply:

> Boy, Jennifer, do I ever need to talk to you!
> Yes, let's have lunch this week. So much
> to make you understand.
>
> B.B.

Jennifer called him right away and left a message for him to phone her. The next day she stood watching the Associated Press wire machine, looking for a Sunday column idea. Often the reporters resented the privileged columnists leaving their offices and getting in the way, so she was careful to stand aside any time anyone approached the machine.

'Hey, Jenn!' rewrite man Dick Harlan called from his desk, phone to his ear. 'You know Block from the *Trib*?'

Several others looked up, annoyed, so Jennifer just nodded and approached Dick, assuming Bobby had finally returned her call.

'Found him dead,' Harlan said.

Jennifer froze while others gathered around Harlan. 'Just a minute,' he said, listening. He hung up. Jennifer couldn't make her legs carry her farther, but she could hear Dick from where she stood.

'Didn't show up for work this morning, but nobody from the *Trib* checked until about noon. They couldn't get an answer, and the landlord said his car was still in the underground garage, so someone went over. His girlfriend had just shown up with the same idea when they got there. She had a key.'

'How'd he die?' someone asked.

'Nobody knows yet. He take drugs, Jenn?'

She shook her head, still rooted to her spot.

'We'll know soon,' Harlan said. 'In time for the fourth edition.'

Jennifer walked stiff-legged back to her office. She phoned Jim. 'I just heard about it,' he said. 'I don't know any more'n you do. You going over there?'

'Is there anything to see?'

'I s'pose. They just found him. Probably haven't even removed the body yet.'

'I guess I will. Jim, this is doing a strange thing to me. I don't know why.'

'It's always tough when you've known someone, Jennifer.'

'I guess so. See you later?'

'We hadn't planned anything tonight. You need to see me?'

'Maybe.'

'Should I stay available?'

'Would you?'

'For you? I'll be here.'

Jennifer fought tears in the car, wondering if it was because of some strange grief over Bobby Block and the frustration of probably never finding out what he wanted to tell her or the gratitude she felt for being loved by someone like Jim. Who knew what Jim might have had planned for tonight? The baseball season had just started; he often had friends in to watch the game on TV.

At Bobby Block's apartment a few blocks away, Jennifer slipped past police lines without a hitch. It had been many months since she'd had to show her press credentials to get in to a crime scene. She nodded to several acquaintances, none of whom spoke.

She had seen Bobby's girl, still a student at Northwestern, only once before. Jennifer almost didn't recognize her now, but Adrienne Eden could have been Bobby's sister. Like him, she was taller and heftier than average.

In jeans and a baggy flannel shirt, her long, curly, black hair a mess, Adrienne sat at the end of the landing, pressing wads of tissues to her eyes as reporters crowded around her. Jennifer decided not to intrude just then. But when she turned to investigate the apartment, Adrienne cursed her in a sob.

'Wonder if you were here earlier today!' she added. 'Little Miss Righteousness!'

Jennifer flushed and ducked into the apartment, wondering if Adrienne could have known about Bobby's note and also realizing that if the other reporters had not known whom Adrienne was addressing, Adrienne would tell them. And now Jennifer found herself not ten feet from the bloated, discoloured body of Robert A. Block, twenty-five, deceased. He was bare-chested and barefoot, wearing pyjama bottoms. Police forensics shot their final photographs, and the Cook County coroner made a few more notes before signalling paramedics to cover the body and lift it on to a trolley.

The medical examiner was taken aback when Jennifer asked what he thought, because she was the only reporter in the room and didn't even have her notebook out. Dr. Jacob Steinmetz recognized her, though.

'Hard to say yet, Miss Grey. Didn't appear to be strangulation, and I found no preliminary signs of poisoning, though he apparently died while eating.'

Jennifer peered past him into the kitchenette where a cold breakfast remained on the table.

'Could have been a heart attack. He carried a
lot of weight for a young man.'

'He couldn't have been murdered?'

'I couldn't say. Don't think so. No sign of foul
play. If it was a poisoning, it was pretty sophisticated. Nothing common anyway. I thought he
had choked on food, but I was wrong. You can
see from the upended chair in there that he
apparently bolted from the table into here and
collapsed. Nasty head wound from hitting the
floor, but I don't think that killed him. I'm guessing he was dead before he hit the floor. We'll see.
If this had happened a few years ago, I'd fear
cyanide — but I doubt it here.'

Other reporters were crowding around. 'I'll
have a statement in a few hours,' Dr. Steinmetz
said. 'Nothing now, thank you.'

Several grumbled about his having talked to a
columnist, but none followed him when he left.
'Why does his girlfriend hate you?' someone
asked.

'I don't know,' Jennifer said, wishing she
could give them a 'No comment' but knowing
how they would despise it. 'I hardly know the
woman.'

'She says you had it in for Block.'

It wasn't a question, so Jennifer didn't
respond.

'That true?' someone asked.

'Of course not.'

'Had you two dated?'

'Don't be silly,' Jennifer said. 'Bobby had
worked for me. You know that. I have nothing
more to say.'

'He was pretty tough on you in the paper. You fire him?'

'No.'

'Who did?'

'My boss. I've finished talking.'

'Why was he fired?'

'Ask my boss.' Jennifer pushed her way through to the lift. The questions continued until she was in her car, and she sensed the frustration of people who were subjected to that regularly. Her one consolation was that none of the three papers in Chicago was a scandal sheet. The reporters asked tough questions to elicit answers, but none would print the screaming headlines of the yellow journalist.

Was Bobby going to apologize for having caused Jennifer so much trouble? Was he going to explain himself, maybe make excuses? Did he know his life was in danger? Jennifer knew she would never know unless she searched for the answers herself.

Back at her office, she phoned the precinct station house to find that a Cap Duffy had been assigned to the case. She didn't recognize the name. 'That a nickname?' she asked.

'I dunno,' the desk sergeant said. 'Prob'ly.'

'Rank?'

'Just a detective.'

'Homicide?'

'Yeah.'

'Who decided this was a homicide?'

'Who's askin', lady? Young, healthy guy croaks at breakfast with no food in his throat. That sounds suspicious to me, homicide or not.

We got to check out the suspicious deaths, right? So who would *you* put on a suspicious death, someone in vice control?'

Jennifer buzzed Dick Harlan.

'Rewrite.'

'Yeah, Dick, Jennifer. Who've you got on the Block death? I didn't see anybody over there.'

'I don't know if anybody's on it yet, Jenn. What were you doing there?'

'I have no restrictions.'

'I know, but you wouldn't write about *that* death, would you?'

'I might. Why not?'

'Well, I mean, I don't know. Just seems sorta tacky, that's all. Forget it, what do I know? You want me to let you know when I find out who Leo assigns?'

'Nah, thanks. I'll ask him.'

'It'll be a tough one to assign, won't it, Jenn?'

'How's that?'

'Just for fairness, we should find someone who didn't go to Medill, shouldn't we?'

'I guess so,' Jennifer said.

'That won't be easy around here.'

'*I* didn't go to Medill.'

'Yeah, but you're a star. And talk about fairness. No way you'll get assigned to this one. If you cover Bobby Block's death, you'll be doing it in your column, not in the news.'

2

'So, what did Leo say?' Jim asked at dinner, reaching for Jennifer's hand across the table.

'He agreed with Harlan.'

'How about you? Don't you agree with Harlan?'

'Of course. But Leo says old man Cooper doesn't want me to deal with it even in my column, and there weren't supposed to be any limitations on my column.'

Jim smiled and straightened as the waiter arrived, and Jennifer watched as he ordered. She had always envied Jim's ability to chat casually with perfect strangers. Usually his rosy complexion and pale blue eyes, offset by almost white blond hair, distracted listeners long enough for him to put them at ease.

When they were alone again, she interrupted her own story to thank Jim again for changing his plans for her.

He brushed it off. 'I'd rather be with you than a bunch of divorced cops or married ones who should be home with their wives, anyway. And it's not as if you haven't done the same for me.'

'But you enjoy relaxing and watching a ball game.'

'More than being with you? Someday I'll prove you wrong about that.'

Jennifer didn't want to pursue *that* statement. If they were married, she'd watch the games with him, and they'd kill both birds with the same stone. But the mention of marriage was not going to come from her lips first. Maybe he didn't want to marry a widow anyway.

From the look in his eyes she would have guessed that indeed he did, and she couldn't help looking forward to his endearing good-bye. She never liked the thought of being apart from him, yet he was so loving, so gentle with her, embracing her as if she were a fragile china doll.

He lit old fires in her, yet he didn't push her, didn't exhibit the urgency that would have scared her off. She found him exciting; she loved him. And she couldn't shake off the crazy feeling that, though the good-bye would mean she would be apart from him again, she longed for the thrill, the beauty, the purity of it.

After their salads came and they had prayed, she asked, 'Do you think Max Cooper has a right to renege on his commitment to my freedom with the column?'

'Absolutely,' Jim said, without hesitation.

It had been a rhetorical question, begging an answer that would allow Jennifer's soliloquy to masquerade as dialogue. Jim's response, of course, brought her up short.

'You *do*?'

'Of course. You believe in freedom of the press, don't you?'

'Ah, yes. But, uh, that was going to be *my* argument, Sweetheart. How does freedom of the press justify Cooper's position and not mine?'

'Freedom of the press belongs to the one who owns the press, not to the ones who are employed by him.'

She sat silent. 'But he promised,' she said finally.

'That's *his* problem. He'll have to live with that. But certainly it's his prerogative to change his mind. And he *does* have a point in this case, Jenn.'

'I was afraid you were going to get around to that,' she said smiling. 'I hate logic.'

They ate in silence, occasionally gazing deep into each other's eyes. Jennifer wondered at herself and how she could unabashedly stare at Jim without even attempting to hide her pleasure in him. The April 21 evening was unseasonably warm, so after dinner they walked to the Oak Street Beach and sat on concrete benches.

'I shouldn't have reacted so impulsively to your question,' Jim said, his arm around her waist. 'You wanted an ear; I gave you a mouth.'

'But you were right, Jim. It's just that I *want* to write about Bobby Block.'

'Why?'

'I haven't thought that through. As soon as I was over the initial shock, I knew I had to get to know him as soon as possible. The sooner he's in the ground, the less chance that I'll know anything about him.'

Jim squinted out at a blinking light a mile off the shore. 'Are you sure there's anything there to know?' he asked. 'Could it be that Block was just one of those selfish types who crash through life, destroying everything and everybody in their way?'

'Maybe.'

'But it's not his death you want to write about?'

'Not really. There was a core of something there, something deeper than what everyone saw. It's what made him a decent police reporter after all, in spite of everything.'

'Decency from indecency, huh? But you can't write about him, Jenn.'

'Why not?'

'The guy in the city room — '

'Harlan?'

'Yeah, he's right. It would be tacky. If you're not investigating the death, you can only write about what you know. You haven't talked with the man for months. The only contact you had with him was unpleasant. He was a scoundrel. He was out to get you. He hurt you, slowed your career, never gave you a chance to fight back or even know where he stood. Is that what you want to print about a dead man?'

Jennifer stood and faced Lake Shore Drive, watching the cars and buses and hearing the tyres and horns. After two years of working in the city, those sounds had become a mere backdrop that no longer abused the senses.

Why did she want to pursue Bobby Block to his grave? Should she feel guilty for not having told him of her faith? She couldn't remember one opportunity. It seemed all she had done in his presence was defend herself or be careful not to implicate herself.

That wasn't it. In fact, Bobby knew where she stood and taunted her for it. It appeared to make him hostile, or threaten him somehow. She had tried not to intentionally turn him off. But he had been turned off anyway.

Jim stood behind her and massaged her shoulders. He said nothing. That was one of the reasons she loved him so. He knew when to counsel, when to talk, when to ask, when to be quiet.

'I know there's nothing I can write about him yet,' she admitted. Jim rested his chin on her shoulder from behind so he could hear her over the din of the traffic. She turned and kissed him, and they walked back to his car.

Instead of letting him open the door for her, however, she leaned back against it and gently drew him to herself. 'How about two good-byes tonight?' she asked.

He raised his eyebrows. 'Hmm?'

'One now — and one at the door,' she said.

'Twist my arm,' he said, kissing her.

'I've got a couple of drawers worth of research on some interesting columns,' she said in the car. 'I'm going to try to bang out three tomorrow before two o'clock. That'll give me a few days to snoop around.'

'Where are you going to snoop?'

'Northwestern.'

'Yeah?' he said, as if making a list and waiting for the next location.

'And Bobby's apartment building.'

'Yeah, OK, that'll be picked over pretty well by the time you get there.'

'His family.'

'Good. And?'

'And?'

'You're leaving out two perfectly logical places.'

'I told you — '

'I know, you hate logic. But you're still logical, so where else will you dig?'

'The *Trib*.'

'I love it.'

'Why?'

'I knew you'd say the *Trib*, but think about it. Think how you'd respond if reporters from the *Sun-Times* waltzed over to research in *your* shop. How would they be received?'

'It wouldn't be a problem, Jim. It really wouldn't. In fact, I think we'd respect them and show them deference. It would be a good chance to show professionalism.'

'Except that you aren't just a reporter, Jenn. And you're not just *any* columnist. You're Block's former boss. You're one of the reasons he was fired. You and he go back a long, shabby way.'

'Meaning?'

'You had a motive to murder the man, Jenn.'

'Come on, Jim.'

'I know, but am I wrong?'

Jennifer stared straight ahead, as if studying the road as Jim pulled into the underground garage beneath her building. 'I don't suppose they'd welcome me with open arms. So what's the other logical place I left out?'

'It's so obvious I'll spare you the embarrassment of telling you.'

'You mean the Police Department?'

'Of course,' Jim said.

'Well, sure, that's why I didn't mention it.' They laughed.

In the lift she asked Jim about the detective with the funny name.

'Yeah, I like Duffy a lot. We were uniformed beat cops together. I rode with him a few times. All he's ever wanted to be in his life was a detective.'

'And he's a good one?'

'Oh, yes. One of the best.'

'But he's not a sergeant or anything like that?'

'Doesn't want to be. Wants to be on the street — hustling, working.'

'Will I like him?'

'Oh, sure. Question is, will he like you?'

Jennifer leaned back against her door and took Jim's hands in hers. 'How could anybody not like me?' she asked, smiling.

He chuckled. 'Cap has never felt comfortable with women.'

'Is he married?'

'Yes, and to the perfect match. He treats her

like a queen, and apparently she doesn't grouse about his crazy hours and his idiosyncrasies.'

'Which are?'

'Just like any career detective. He's *always* on a case. Any time of the day or night, talking about it, making calls, running here and there.'

'A woman would really have to trust a man like that.'

'Oh, and she does. When you meet him, you'll know he's trustworthy. It's written all over him.'

'Children?'

'Nope.'

'Interesting.'

'That he is.'

'Would he be working tonight?'

'Probably. Until he knows how Block died. Why?'

'Then I'm still working.'

'Jenn, you're tired. You're not really going out again tonight, are you?'

'No, but I can call him, can't I?'

'Incurable,' Jim said, shaking his head. And he kissed her good night a second time. Maybe next time, she decided, she'd try for three good-byes.

'Chicago Police.'

'Detective Duffy, please.'

'Who may I say is calling?'

'Jennifer Grey, *Chicago Day*.'

'Oh, hi, Miss Grey. Cap's on the street. Want me to have him call you?'

She gave him her private number at the *Day*. Then she called the night wire editor and asked if he would programme the phone in Jennifer's office to ring at her apartment number, which Jennifer never publicized to outsiders.

She was nearly asleep an hour later when her phone rang.

'Jennifer Grey?'

'Who's calling, please?' she said.

'Duffy.'

'Oh, yes! Mr. Duffy, how are you?'

'I'm, uh, fine, ma'am. How are you?'

'Fine, fine. Can we get together?'

'I don't think so. What can I do for you?'

'I'm calling regarding Robert Block. Have you determined the cause of death?'

'Well, that's not for me to determine, ma'am. That's up to the —'

'I know, Mr. Duffy. Has the medical examiner determined the cause of death?'

'Momentarily.'

'Pardon me?'

'I'm calling from his office. We're expecting his statement any minute.'

'Would you mind very much calling me with it?'

'Well, I don't know. If it's what I think it's going to be, I may be pretty busy.'

'Keeping track of suspects?'

'Ma'am?'

'You know what I mean, Detective Duffy. The only thing you think it could be that would keep you busy would be murder. Why are you thinking it might be murder?'

'Well, not specifically murder.'

'What else would concern you?'

23

'Well, manslaughter, justifiable homicide, stuff like that.'

'But you're saying that you think it's probably a suspicious death, so —'

'Well, any death is suspicious until it's explained.'

'I know, I know,' Jennifer said, exasperated. Maybe Duffy was more charming in person. 'Can you tell me why it might be a death of other than natural causes?'

'You mean besides the fact that the man was only twenty-five years old?'

'Yes.'

'No.'

'No?'

'No.'

'Why not?'

'Because I'm afraid you would be one of the suspects, ma'am, and frankly, you're the only one who's tried to reach *me* tonight.'

Jennifer smiled, but kept from laughing. 'I imagine I am,' she said.

'Can you tell me the approximate time of death?'

'Not until I get your alibis, ma'am.'

'Uh-huh. And I don't suppose you want those by phone.'

'Not unless you want to give them to me.'

'No,' she said, not wanting to miss the privilege of meeting this man. 'When and if the M.E. decides the cause of death, you know where to find me. But let me get a good night's sleep first, OK?'

'You won't be going anywhere?'

'Of course not.'

'I may regret it, but I'm going to believe you, because you're such a visible person.'

'Thank you.'

'And because you're a friend of Jim Purcell.'

'That's the real reason you trust me, isn't it?'

'Yes, ma'am,' Duffy said, almost apologetically.

'He's the best credential I've got, even with my picture on the front page of the paper every day.'

'Yes, ma'am.'

'Tell me something. Block died this morning while eating breakfast, right?'

'I'd rather interview you before we get into that, ma'am.'

'I was there, Mr. Duffy. I saw him in his pyjamas.'

'Alive?'

'Of course not.'

'But we might have found your prints in the apartment?'

'I'm not that careless after all these years. No, if you found unidentified prints in the apartment, unless they were on the arm of the medical examiner's coat, they aren't mine. You'll call me in the morning?'

'Yes, ma'am.'

3 The next morning on her way to work, Jennifer heard a radio report from Coroner Steinmetz. He had determined the cause of Bobby's death as a slow, timed poison that could have entered the bloodstream as early as eighteen to twenty-four hours before he died.

In her office, Jennifer felt strangely distracted as she hunched over a two-drawer file and studied research on the three columns she hoped to finish by mid-afternoon.

This was the second time in her brief career with the *Day* that she'd been a possible suspect in a murder case — someone who had been in close enough proximity to the victim that she could not be ruled out without at least a hasty investigation.

Jennifer sensed someone in the doorway of her office and looked up into the wryly smiling face of City Editor Leo Stanton. He had his usual early morning look. Brown wing-tipped shoes, pleated and perfectly seamed dark brown woollen slacks, powder blue shirt — already unbuttoned at the neck — with a slightly loosened blue and brown club tie of just the right width, and a beige slipover.

Leo was classic, natty-but-casual, and only the ever-present unlit cigar spoiled the effect. He had removed it from his lips so he could grin at Jennifer, but the sight of a well-dressed middle-aged man of success with a soggy cigar in his hand almost made Jennifer choke.

No one who liked the boss ever criticized him for his pacifier, and she liked him. She returned his smile.

'So how's my perennial murder suspect this morning?'

'I'm all right, Leo. How'd you know?'

'You must have your phone turned off or something. A detective has been calling and getting no answer, and he's afraid you've left town.'

'Oh, no,' she said, quickly reprogramming her phone.

'Not to worry. I told him you were here.'

'Is he coming?'

'No. Wants you to come there.'

'Where's there?'

'Chicago Avenue Precinct Station.' Jennifer started to assemble her things. 'You've got time,' Leo added. 'You're supposed to be there at eleven. Anyway, don't I get to hear this story first?'

She pointed to a magazine-stacked chair. Leo lifted the stack and sat, holding the magazines in

his lap. 'What do you want to hear, Leo? You
know I don't kill people.'

He put his left hand on top of the magazines
for balance and returned the cigar to his mouth,
jamming it between his teeth and the inside of
his cheek so only half of it still showed. It left
him remarkably articulate.

'You can't tell me you wouldn't have been
tempted a time or two to do away with Bobby
Block.'

'Leo, you know me better than that. I get angry
with people, sure, and Bobby drove me crazy.
But no, I never once thought of injuring the kid,
let alone killing him.' She had decided not to tell
Leo about the note. At least not yet.

Leo grinned at her.

'You don't believe me?' she said.

''Course I do. I was just thinking that *I* often
thought of injuring him.'

Jennifer fell silent, remembering the storied
battles between the undisputed expert veteran of
the staff and the know-it-all upstart from Medill
who liked to preface his remarks with, 'If I was
running the city room — '

'Maybe *you* should be a suspect,' Jennifer said
finally.

Leo smiled again, then appeared deep in
thought, the smile fading. 'It's really sad, isn't it?'
he said. 'I can't say I've missed Block since we let
him go, but it's weird to think that he's dead.'

'Dead is one thing,' Jennifer said. 'Poisoned is
something else.'

'And he had done quite a job for the *Tribune*,
hadn't he?' Leo said, as if he hadn't heard her.

'You wish you'd kept him and let *me* go?'

That brought Leo back. He turned to stare at her. 'You kidding?'

They each looked down and said nothing. Leo stood and replaced the magazines. A short laugh sneaked from his throat. 'Think of where we'd be now,' he said. He moved to the door but stopped and turned on his way out. 'If you want to talk when you get back, I'll be here.'

'Thanks, Leo. I'm going to want to finish a couple of more columns today to give me a little breather.'

He squinted at her. 'You never needed a breather in your life. What are you up to?'

'I just want time to do my own snooping on this thing.'

'Why?'

Jennifer stood and sat on top of her cluttered desk. 'I don't know, Leo. Block intrigues me somehow. I could never get next to him. You know how you usually know, or think you know, what someone's problem is?'

Leo nodded.

'With Bobby, I never knew. I thought I did. I guessed ambition, jealousy, that type of thing.'

'Me too,' Leo said. 'I still think so.'

'I don't. There was something more there.' She wondered if she would have thought so, had she not received the note.

Leo looked at his watch. 'You've got an hour before you have to see the detective,' he said. 'You got another minute for me?'

He shut the door. This time he put the magazines on the floor and leaned forward as he sat, elbows on his knees, eyes intense. 'I've got to admit something to you, Jennifer. It doesn't surprise me that you want to get into this case and probably write about it, am I right?'

She nodded.

'You also know how that would look?'

'I've been told by many people.'

'Not by me,' he said.

'No, but you're about to tell me I can't do it.'

'Not necessarily. But you're going to have to take a different approach.'

'Different from what, Leo? I haven't said anything about how I might do it.'

'You forget that I know you, Jenn. If I had to guess, you'd either write about having worked with him and you'd hint about a troubling aspect of his personality, one you admit you have not fathomed out —'

Jennifer started to speak, but Leo continued, 'or you'd write about how shocking and unsettling it is to know someone who has been robbed of life at a prime age. Those are old saws, Jenn, tearjerkers. And it doesn't take a top-notch columnist to do them. They're too easy.'

'Well, you don't have to believe me, Leo, but that's not the approach I was going to take.'

She told him of her plan to poke around the *Trib,* Block's apartment building, Northwestern, and the Police Department.

Leo shook his head. 'Your strength is also your curse, Jenn. You've become too visible to be effective as an investigative reporter. Forget it.'

Jennifer wasn't entirely convinced, but she'd heard it so many times she was beginning to waver. 'You said you weren't going to tell me I couldn't do it. What's the new approach, the one you think *would* work?'

'You like to write continuing pieces as opposed to one-shot deals like you're trying to bat out today, right?'

She nodded.

'Cover the investigation. You always hear from cops that you learn more about someone's life from studying his death than you'd learn from him when he was alive.'

Jennifer thought for a moment. 'But that's been overdone too, hasn't it? The highly descriptive pieces about dingy station houses and scruffy cops who work around the clock?'

'So do it fresh,' Leo said. 'Give it the perspective of a woman who knew the victim. And avoid the clichés. You don't know if this detective is interesting or not.'

'Jim thinks he is, but the guy wouldn't win any personality contests, at least based on our phone conversation last night.'

'He's got an interesting name,' Leo said. 'You've got to give him that. Duffy. But why would they put a captain on this investigation?'

'He's not a captain.'

'I thought he told me he was Captain Duffy from Homicide.'

'No. *Cap* Duffy. He's not even a sergeant.'

'I'm intrigued already. You?'

'I thought Cooper said I couldn't write about Block.'

'I've already talked to him about this. You want to do it or not?'

'Of course I do. And thanks, Leo.'

'You kickin' me out?'

'Hm?'

'That was a conversation-ending *thanks*, Jenn.'

'Since when does the employee kick out the employer, Leo?'

'When the employee becomes as important to the paper as the City Editor, that's when.'

'I appreciate that, Leo, but I'm not taking this visible celebrity thing seriously. I know who I am, and you know you're the brains behind my column, so don't think I'll ever get uppity about it. You taught me everything I know and gave me the confidence to do what I'm doing.'

Leo stood, smiling a tight-lipped smile. 'And don't you forget it,' he said. 'Seriously, Jennifer, that was nice. Do you really believe that?'

Jennifer grinned mischievously. 'No, but it seemed like the right thing to say at the time.'

'Ooh, you're bad,' Leo said, pointing at her.

She stood and opened the door.

'Now you *are* kicking me out,' he said.

'You got that right.'

As he passed her she added seriously, 'You know what's really good about this? I despise writing timeless columns that could run any time, even if getting ahead does free me up a little.'

'I know what you mean. Your column needs that daily freshness. And if people get hooked on one of your angles, they'll stay with you for a week or even two on the same topic. This should be worth at least that.'

At 10.50 a.m. Jennifer announced herself at the desk of the Chicago Avenue Precinct station. She was directed to sit on an oily wooden bench across from an identical one, on which was heavily settled an elderly woman, dressed as if for winter.

The woman wore dark, thick horn-rimmed glasses under a heavy scarf tied around her head. She wore a thick overcoat and stumpy rubber boots, flanked on either side by twine-handled carrier-bags, both worn thin, but one ironically bearing the name of an exclusive shop in Water Tower Place. Jennifer wondered if the woman had been arrested for shoplifting or was just waiting for someone.

Jennifer tried to smile at the old woman, who stared straight ahead, as if seeing nothing, sleeping with her eyes open. Soon another woman, not as heavy but similarly dressed, trudged from the tile corridor and stood by her.

Without acknowledging her companion's presence, Rubber Boots slowly stood, grasped her bags, and wandered out to the front door with her friend. Jennifer's eyes followed them out, and when she turned back around, a seedy looking man had taken the woman's place on the opposite bench.

Jennifer had planned to kill her waiting time by making up stories about the women and the dastardly thing they might have done to result in their being hauled in by the police. But this man would be even more interesting to use as fiction fodder.

He was reading the racing form on the sports page, and Jennifer wondered if he had ever won a dime. He was thin and small, perhaps wiry, and he appeared down on his luck.

When she was sure he was deep into the fine print, she checked him out carefully. He wore thick-soled, soft fabric shoes; short, dark green, double-knit, polyester slacks that reached the tops of his ankles and revealed thin, light green socks with yellow triangles and elastic tops that had been through a hot dryer one time too many. A dingy dark green and off-white sports coat peeked out from under the bottom of a corduroy car coat, one of those with toggles that poke through any remaining unbroken leatherette loops. It had zippered pockets, one of which still looked zippable.

His face was thin and pointed, and he had a cleft both in his chin and between his nostrils. His lips were a little too generous for his small mouth, and he had large, sad, grey eyes that were slightly bloodshot and peered out at the paper over puffy bags.

He appeared about ten days overdue for a haircut, with curly wisps showing from behind his neck. His sideburns were not only a fraction too long, but also curling up in the middle. Jennifer wondered why his hair wasn't greasy, for it didn't seem to fit in with the rest of his appearance. His hands also were clean, and he was clean shaven.

Beside him on the bench was a hat that appeared to match his tie. It was pale green with yellow and brown plaid.

She looked at her watch and decided that if Detective Duffy was on time, she would have about a minute to guess Green and Brown's story. She was daydreaming a tale about his having lost his wallet at the racetrack and having come in to see if anyone had turned it in, when she realized he was looking at her from over the top of his newspaper.

Jennifer quickly looked away and ran her fingers between the back of her neck and her hair. When she stole a glance back at him, he was still looking at her, and she hoped she hadn't offended him by staring at him for so long.

She started to look away again, but she noticed him reach to the inside breast pocket of his sports coat and produce a pair of half glasses. He put them on and began digging through the paper.

She wondered why he needed his glasses to pore through the paper when he hadn't worn them to study the racing charts. He turned to the front page, and she noticed he was reading the *Day*. He folded it up so that her column and her mug shot stared out at him.

Did he recognize her? He looked at the column photo and then at her over the tops of his spectacles. Jennifer couldn't fight a blush as she nodded to acknowledge his gaze. He carefully placed the paper beneath his hat on the bench, ceremoniously took off his glasses, and replaced them in his pocket.

He clapped a palm on each of his knees and leaned forward, peering intently into Jennifer's eyes. 'Jennifer Grey?' he asked in an almost sweet, mellow voice that didn't seem to fit.

She nodded again with an apologetic smile.

He reached to shake her hand and she slowly, cautiously complied.

'I'm Cap Duffy,' he said, rising.

4 Jennifer couldn't suppress an amazed expression, which made Duffy smile. 'I'm sorry, but I often do this,' he said. 'I have trouble meeting people, so I just sit with them and get used to them first.'

'Bizarre,' she managed, and followed him back to his cubbyhole.

He cleared a place for her to sit, then stepped over her to the rickety chair wedged in behind his desk, which was jammed against one wall. The room was not built for two. 'Be glad my partner's off today,' Duffy said, then laughed. 'Just kidding. I work alone.'

'That's unusual, isn't it?'

'Nah. Some of us don't look like cops unless there's two of us. I can pass for anything, right?' Jennifer almost nodded. 'But if I'm hangin' around with a guy in a trench coat and rubber-soled shoes with a bulge at his hip, then all of a sudden we both might as well be wearin' uniforms, you follow me?'

Duffy wrenched off his car coat without standing and let it drape over the back of his chair. Jennifer did the same. As the detective dug in a file drawer for the case folder, she spoke.

'Forgive my reporter's curiosity. I know why I'm here and that you have a lot of questions to ask me, but could I ask you one first?'

'Sure.'

'I'm intrigued by your name.'

'Duffy? It's French.'

Jennifer laughed.

Duffy straightened up and stared at her, a hint of a smile at his lips. 'You got somethin' against the French?' he said.

'No, I was curious about your first name.'

'You don't know my first name.'

'It's Cap, isn't it?'

'You ever hear anybody go by the name of *Cap?*'

'Well, no, that's why I asked. That *is* your name, isn't it?'

'If you've never heard of anybody going by that name, then it's not my name, is it?'

'OK,' she said, 'I'll bite. What's your *real* first name?'

'Would a guy who goes by Cap to hide his real name wanna *tell* his real name?' Duffy was smiling broadly now. 'Ah, I never was any good at games. My name is Harold.'

'There's nothing wrong with the name Harold.'

'I hate it.'

'I don't.'

'Then *you* can use it.'

'I thought you were supposed to be shy with women.'

'Who told you that? I'm not saying I'm not, but who told you? Oh, I know. That big mouth boyfriend of yours.'

'So, where'd the name Cap come from?'

'I always wear one, that's all.'

Jennifer sat smiling at Cap Duffy. She wanted to ask him if the rest of his ensemble was a put-on as well, but she didn't dare. He *could* use the clothes as sort of a Columbo facade, hiding the brilliant mind and all that. Then again, he could just be a cop with no sense of fashion.

Duffy suddenly grew serious, acting as if he wished they'd saved the informal banter until she'd been cleared. 'I have several questions to ask you, if you don't mind.'

'Not at all,' she said.

'Do you wish to have a lawyer present?'

'Should I?'

'It's entirely up to you.'

'Am I under arrest?'

'No, ma'am. If you were under arrest, I would read you your rights.'

'I know. Why did you ask about a lawyer?'

'Just a suggestion.'

'*Might* I be placed under arrest?'

'That's always a possibility. If your answers don't satisfy me or I can't corroborate them, I may be forced to arrest you, yes.'

'Do you think it's possible that I murdered Bobby Block?'

'I've learned to never label anything an *impos*-sibility, let me put it that way.'

'Well, fine then,' she said, her heart pounding as she wondered if something in Duffy's investigation had already revealed that she and Block had been trying to get together for some time and that he had, in fact, written to her the day before he died. 'Just ask your questions.'

'I didn't mean to offend you, Miss Grey.'

'*Mrs.* Grey.'

'Excuse me, Mrs. Grey. You're married?'

'Widowed.'

'I'm sorry.'

'So am I.'

'Mrs. Grey, I wasn't trying to offend you. I always suggest a lawyer as a courtesy. If I didn't think it was possible you had anything to do with Block's death, I wouldn't have asked you to come here. I'd love to be able to clear you, if for no other reason than to streamline my work. I don't need suspects all over town.'

Jennifer was ashamed for having reacted so sharply, but she said nothing.

'Now, if I may begin. How long did you know the deceased?'

'I saw him around, knew who he was, ever since my first week on the staff of the *Day*, about two years ago. Then when I was assigned to the police beat about a year ago, I became his supervisor.'

'How would you characterize your relationship?'

'Stormy.'

Jennifer told him the whole story of Bobby's antagonism, his backstabbing, his deviousness.

Duffy made detailed notes in a delicate script as she spoke.

'I know I haven't done myself any good by telling you this,' she said, still holding her breath over the note.

'Honesty never hurts.'

'Except that if I didn't believe I was supposed to love my enemies and pray for those who despitefully use me, what I just told you might have given me a motive for murder.'

Duffy smiled, and it was apparent to Jennifer that, for a moment, his mind was miles away. 'Yes,' he said absent-mindedly, 'I suppose it might have.' His eyes stared past her, and he appeared deep in thought. 'Love your enemies, huh?' He smiled again. 'That's the Bible, isn't it?'

She nodded, not wanting to bring him back from this strange reverie. 'That was a memory verse we had to learn in holiday Bible school,' he said. 'Thirty years ago.' He grunted as if remembering the good old days.

Jennifer wanted to press, to find out if he was a Christian, but she decided this wasn't the time.

'You believe that, Mrs. Grey?'

'Yes.'

'That's good. That's no defence, but that's good. I believe you.'

'You believe I'm innocent?'

'Well, no, it's a little early for that. I just believe that you believe that you're supposed to love your enemies and pray for them. Whether you practised that with Robert Block, I'm not sure yet. Can you tell me your general whereabouts beginning Tuesday at the end of your workday?'

'Sure. I worked a little late finishing my column for Wednesday. Then I had to hurry home because I entertained my parents from Rockford and Jim, and I was expecting them at seven.'

'You say that as if they didn't show up at seven.'

'Well, they didn't. I did some fast grocery shopping, and by the time I got home just before six-thirty they were all already there and waiting outside. I was going to throw on some steaks and toss a salad, but my father insisted on taking us to dinner at Carson's.'

'And then?'

'Back to my place for dessert.'

'And they left when?'

'About eleven.'

'And you didn't leave your apartment until the next morning when you left for work?'

'Correct.'

'Do you remember Wednesday?'

'Of course; what do you mean?'

'The details. Where you went during the workday, that type of thing.'

'I spent the morning on the phone with the mayor's press secretary, explaining why I had never written a column on the mayor and warning that if I *did* write one, it might be critical.'

'This is off the subject, Mrs. Grey, but I'm curious. Why might it be critical?'

'No reason. I have nothing against the mayor. That's why I've never written a column about the mayor. But if I wrote one now, it would have to be about a press secretary who seeks favourable publicity.'

'That *is* kinda base, isn't it?'

Jennifer nodded. 'I went to lunch with Max Cooper and Leo Stanton at Hunan's.'

'And they are?'

'Cooper is the publisher of the *Day*, and Stanton is my boss, the City Editor.'

'No, I know. I mean, who are the Hunans?'

'That's a Chinese restaurant. The House of Hunan, Michigan Avenue.'

'Good?'

'Great.'

'OK, after that?'

'Ah, let's see. Oh, yes. I went to Cabrini-Green where I talked with a Miss Hawkins about an opinion piece she had had printed in *Time* magazine. Made a good Friday column. You've seen it.'

'Excuse me?'

'You may not have read it, but that's what you were looking at when you were pretending to be someone else out there.'

'I wasn't pretending. I — '

'Whatever. You might want to read it.'

'I probably will. How long were you with this Hawkins woman?'

'About three hours, until four o'clock.'

'All that time for that short column?'

'You *did* read it!'

'Of course. It takes that long to get column material?'

'Sometimes more, sometimes less. There has to be more than you see in the paper every day.'

'I guess so.'

'Then I went back to the office for a few minutes, then home to get ready for prayer meeting.'

'Prayer meeting?'

'Yes, Jim and I go together whenever he's off on Wednesday nights.' She felt guilty now, because it was while she was back in the office for those few minutes that she had received the note from Bobby. She wondered how long she could go on telling Cap Duffy about loving her enemies and going to prayer meetings when she was withholding evidence in a murder case.

'And where is this?'

'At his church in Waukegan.'

'Uh-huh. Prayer meeting. And then?'

'Out for a snack with another couple, the Barbers, and then home.'

'He stay with you?'

'Excuse me?'

'Purcell stay with you?'

'Never.'

'Never?'

'No, sir. We'll have plenty of time together some day. Please don't tell him I said that.'

Duffy grinned. 'And you were in all night until work the next morning?'

Jennifer nodded. 'And then I was in the news-room after lunch when I heard about Bobby.'

'And you weren't gone from the office Thurs-day morning before that?'

'No.'

'Went straight to work?'

'Yes.'

'Out for lunch?'

'No, someone went for sandwiches.'

'When was the last time you saw Bobby Block alive?'

'I saw him in January at a Chicago Press Club luncheon.'

'Talk to him?'

'Tried to.'

'Said hi and got no response?'

'Not even that much. I waved to him from across the room. He didn't acknowledge me. I moved toward him, and he moved away.'

'That the last time?'

'I think so. No, I saw him at a Police Department press conference about a month later. Just from a distance. No contact.' She pressed her lips together. News of the note was ready to burst from her, but she decided to hold it as long as she could. She didn't know why. It wasn't to protect herself. She knew better than that. It was just that this part of it was hers. It was the reason *she* wanted to investigate Bobby's death for herself.

Duffy sat staring at her. 'I have a lot of people to talk to before I clear you,' he said. He began reading from his list. 'Your parents, Jim, the mayor's press secretary, Cooper and/or Stanton, Miss Hawkins, the Barbers, the doorman at your apartment, and the receptionist in your office.'

'You have to talk to my parents?'

'Just routine. I do it in such a way that they don't worry.'

'I don't suppose I can tail you around on this case for a week's worth of columns until I've been cleared myself.'

'You got that right. Anyway, who said you could do that?'

'My boss.'

'Don't *I* have any say in it?'

'Of course.'

'I couldn't let you do that.'

'Not even for a friend of Jim's?'

'What would my sergeant say?'

'What will *my* boss say? When Bob Greene runs out of column material over at the *Trib*, he writes about what it's like to shave with a razor for the first time at age thirty-five. Don't push me to that kind of fluff. If you're a good cop, it can only be good publicity, right? That's what the cops need right now, just like the mayor.'

'Yeah, and I don't even have a press secretary begging for it. Listen, I'll think about it. But meanwhile, you stay outta my hair and stay accessible. I'm hoping for your sake that your story checks out.'

'How long will that take?'

'Not long. I've got a lot of other suspects. This guy had very few friends, you know.'

'He had a girlfriend.'

'How well I know. She's a suspect too.'

'Adrienne?'

'Excuse me?'

'Adrienne Eden is a suspect?'

'That's not the name I have down here.' He rifled through his notebook. 'I'm eager to talk to a Josie Sisk.'

'You've got names I haven't got, and I've got names you haven't got. We could be good for each other, Mr. Duffy.'

'Call me Cap.'

5 Back at her office, Jennifer worked on the first of her undated columns, just in case Duffy decided that — even if cleared — he didn't want her dogging his every move during the investigation. He seemed so strange, she couldn't even predict what he would decide when Leo and Max Cooper visited and asked.

'What really ices my cake,' the old publisher said in mock exasperation, 'is that every time I turn around, you're a suspect in a murder case!'

'This is only the second time,' Jennifer said weakly, sending Cooper into a fit of laughter.

'Lemme know when you've been cleared,' he said. 'Anything we can do for you?'

'I'd like more information about the medical aspects of the death, but I don't want to step on anyone's toes in the newsroom.'

Cooper nodded quickly to Leo who called in a

secretary outside Jennifer's glassed-in office. 'Yes, sir?'

'Stephanie, I want you to get me photocopies of everything we've got on the Block murder so far, and I mean *everything*. Reporters' notes, articles, sidebars, printed statements, wire copy, stuff from the City News Bureau, everything. Just tell 'em it's for me, and I want it ASAP. OK?'

'Certainly.'

'Thanks, Leo,' Jennifer said. 'And thank you, Mr. Cooper.'

'Don't mention it,' Leo said. 'Just be sure to give credit for anything you use. A hot quote or note from a reporter shows up in your column with no attribution, and we'll both be skinned.'

'And rightly so,' Cooper added.

'I've got one more big problem,' Jennifer said. 'I can't concentrate on anything but the murder. If I don't get this general column done and Duffy doesn't let me write about his investigation, I'll have no column for the Sunday edition.'

'You want me to pull a few strings at Police Headquarters?' old man Cooper asked. 'I hate to do it, but I would.'

'No, I hate that type of thing too. The mayor's office tried to do it this morning, asking for a favourable column.'

Cooper swore. 'You oughta call the scoundrel back and tell 'im you'll think about it if he can get you permission to cover the murder investigation!'

'I'd rather do it without any obligations.'

'You wouldn't *have* any! All you're tellin' 'im

47

is that you'll think about it! You wouldn't actually do it!'

Jennifer smiled sympathetically, bringing the old timer back to his senses. 'Listen to me,' he said hoarsely, 'goin' on like a senile, old fool. Well, I'll tell ya, Grey, I want a column from you in Sunday's rag as usual. I'd like it to be the first in your series on this murder investigation, but if it can't be, it can't be. If not, you'll have to come up with something else, and if it's not this afternoon, just make the deadline. Got it?'

'Yes, sir.'

That was all Jennifer needed to take her mind off any alternative column and dig into the material which was soon delivered by Stephanie. She'd hear from Duffy in time to pull off a last minute column, if necessary. Meanwhile, she had homework to do in case his answer was good news.

After about forty-five minutes of poring over the material, Jennifer tried to get the coroner on the phone. It wasn't easy. He had gone home.

Even at his home number, she had to go through a receptionist and an assistant, both of whom were reluctant to believe that she had learned the phone number from the good doctor himself. But she finally got through.

'I'm in the steam room,' she heard him shout over a hissing noise. 'So I was wrong about the poison, what else is new? You gonna fry me on the front page for it?'

'No,' she laughed. 'I've missed a few guesses in my day too. Just tell me about it, and I'll never breathe a word to anyone that you first thought it wasn't a poisoning.'

'Well, Jennifer, the best I can determine, Block was done in by what my toxicological friends call a cumulative poison.'

'Which means?'

'Which means that it was basically an irritant which probably entered the body as a liquid.'

'But not through the mouth?'

'I was getting to that, but how did you know?'

'Just guessing that an irritant would injure the mouth, and you would have seen evidence of that when you did the preliminary examination of the body yesterday.'

'Very good, Jennifer.'

'But what do you mean *cumulative*, Jake? He had to get several doses or something?'

'No. The first dosage could have been enough, but it may have been in such a diluted solution that it would have been absorbed gradually. I suppose it's possible that he received increased dosages and that they finally took their toll, but this appears to me like a whizbang type of reaction to a time bomb sort of poison.'

'For which you as yet have no name?'

'That's right. I saw no evidence of alcohol, barbiturates, or anything like that.'

'How would a poison like that get into his system?'

'Well, of course, that's not for me to say. I did a quick study of the body to look for hypodermic holes. Just below his right hip there's about a one-inch square area that seems to at one time have been punctured repeatedly. Now he could have sat on something, or it could have been a series of injections, maybe all at once, maybe in his sleep.'

'What are you saying?'

'I'm saying I don't know, and I don't want to speculate. I would not term this a suicide by any stretch of the imagination. The man could have been given an injection while he slept, but he would have had to have been a very sound sleeper to sleep through even one such injection, unless a surface anesthetic was applied. I found no evidence of that either.'

'Jake, how will you find out just what the substance was and the effect it had?'

Dr. Steinmetz laughed ruefully. 'I'm afraid we're already aware of the effect, girl.'

'You know what I mean, Jake. What did it actually do to him to kill him?'

'Well, the big job now is left to the serologists. They have to separate the poison from the normal body fluids and purify it so they can fully identify it. Tomorrow a couple of pathology experts and I will be studying the injury the poison inflicted on the tissues of the major vital organs. This poison acted almost as a narcotic when it finally took effect, affecting the organs and resulting in respiratory and circulatory failure. The way he bolted from his chair and probably died before he hit the floor made me expect to find traces of botulin toxin in his mouth.'

'That would have killed him that quickly?'

'Oh, yes. The most potent form of bacterial

toxin causes acute food poisoning that can kill you if you get it past your lips.'

'Could that be caused by bad food?'

'Unlikely. The cases of botulin toxin deaths I've studied have been deliberate poisonings. Every one.'

'But there was no trace of that here?'

'No. But the effect was the same. This, based on what I know right now, was a cumulative poison that exploded upon his system when it was ready. And, as I said at the press conference this morning, it could have entered his bloodstream as long as eighteen to twenty-four hours before death.'

'Thanks so much for making time for me, Jake.'

'Any time, Jenn. Remember our bargain. I gave you a lot more than anyone else in town knows by now.'

'Only because I tracked you down and caught you after you'd done more examining.'

'True, true. But you're still gonna uphold your end, aren't you?'

'Sure. I'm writing the headline right now, Jake. How's this sound: "Coroner Blows Another Diagnosis"?'

'Funny, Jennifer. Good-bye.'

'You like that?'

'Good-bye, Jennifer.'

'It'll be in Sunday's paper.'

'Good-bye, Jennifer.'

'Good-bye, Jake. Thanks again.'

She hung up smiling, glad for some comic relief in such a grisly assignment.

Stephanie appeared at the door, and Jennifer

waved her in. 'There's a Duffy guy in the lobby asking to see you. Should I let him come up? The receptionist says he looks like one of those crazy people who likes to get written up in the paper.'

I wish, Jennifer thought. 'Yeah, send him up,' she said.

Her lower back tingled as she waited and wondered if she was as excited about being cleared as she was about whether Duffy knew about her note from Bobby. Or whether he would allow her to tag along, regardless.

She hadn't noticed before how smoothly Cap Duffy moved. He switched his hat from one hand to the other as he came through the door, sat without making a sound, crossed his legs, and settled back expectantly.

Jennifer stacked her papers neatly and entwined her fingers on top of the desk, leaning forward to give full attention. It seemed to be what Duffy had been waiting for. 'I have good news and bad news,' he said seriously.

'The good news is I've been cleared,' she guessed. 'My references were not only able to corroborate my whereabouts, but they also sang my praises so that you wondered why I didn't go into full-time church work.'

'Right, Joan of Arc.'

'I sometimes wonder that myself.'

'The bad news, however — '

'I know,' she said. 'The bad news is that you don't think you want me along on the investigation.'

'Wrong.'

'Really? I can?'

'No, you can't. But it's not that I don't *think* I want you along; I *know* I don't want you along.'

Jennifer looked hurt.

'I didn't mean to be cold about that,' he said. 'It's just that I know how persistent you newspaper types are, and I needed to be able to shut the door on that little foray into loophole land you just tried to make.'

'Pardon me?'

'When you said I didn't *think* I wanted you to go. That made it sound tentative, as if you still had some say in it, which you don't.'

'You're not trying to sound mean?'

'No, ma'am, I'm truly not.'

'That's good. I'd hate to be on the other end when you're working at it.'

'I'm sorry.'

'So am I. Why does this conversation sound familiar?'

''Cause we had it this morning.'

'Aren't you going to miss this, Mr. Duffy?'

'Call me — '

'I'm sorry, Cap. Aren't you going to miss this?'

'Miss what?'

'Our ease of conversation. You've got to admit you don't get much stimulating conversation in a day's work.'

'I get more than I want. All I do all day is talk to people.'

'But you're not with them long enough to develop a relationship, to be able to volley back and forth with them. C'mon, I know I've stopped conniving and gone to begging, but you know you'd enjoy it. I want to know how you work, where you look, what you're after. Most of all, why.'

Duffy looked at her with his head cocked, apparently unimpressed. 'You really want to get into the *why?*' he asked, incredulously.

'Sure, what did you think?'

'There are lots of whats and hows and whos and wheres, if I remember Intro to Journalism one-oh-one.'

'You know *why* is part of all that, Cap.'

'Yeah, but not the *real* why.'

'I would want to get into that. It would be a major part of what I'd want to say. Why does a man give himself to the kind of work you do? What motivates him? What keeps him sane? What keeps him straight? What keeps him from becoming a cynic?'

Duffy sat thinking, but Jennifer had not the slightest inkling that she was winning him over.

'Well, that's encouraging,' he said, 'but no. You'd want no restrictions, no rules, no letting me see what you write before you print it.'

'That's right,' she said, almost wishing she didn't have to say it if it was going to determine whether she got to work with him. But she'd never forgive herself if she gave away her integrity and credibility.

'No, I'm afraid you'd put off my best leads, scare them, keep them from talking.'

'I'd stay in the car when you talk to people at the *Trib*, if that's what you mean.'

'But how about with Adrienne Eden?'

'You didn't even know about Adrienne before I put you onto her,' Jennifer said.

54

'I would've got to her. He was two-timing her, after all.'

'Really? See, I didn't know that.'

'But she's got no love for you.'

'OK, I'll stay in the background for that one too. But you'd have to tell me what she says.'

'No, you're not going.'

'Cap, you'll wish you'd let me.'

'I will, huh? Gimme a reason.'

'I've given you a bunch.'

'Give me one reason that I'll wish I'd let you.'

'Because I know lots of stuff and lots of people.'

'Like what?'

She told him what she knew about the toxicologists and serologists and pathologists. She spoke quickly and clearly about what she thought they might find and what it would mean. Duffy's wheels were turning. She was giving him so much more than he had learned from the coroner earlier in the day.

He stood and thrust his hands deep into his coat pockets. She knew the time had come. She showed him the note. He read silently, but he took so long she knew he was going over it several times.

'I'm not too thrilled about this,' he said without looking up.

'I know, and I'm sorry. And I swear it's the only thing I've held back from you.'

He scowled at the note. 'You'll be quiet when I'm interviewing people?'

She nodded enthusiastically.

'You won't ask me any questions in front of anyone?'

She shook her head.

'You won't interview my people. You'll stay out of the way when I say to. You'll let me be off-the-record when I say so. You won't call me at home. You'll give me every bit of information you dig up that I haven't come to yet.'

She nodded like a little kid who realized her wish had been granted if she'd just agree to all the rules.

'Jim said you'd agree to everything if I held out long enough,' he said.

'Ooh, you're kidding,' she said. 'He told you that?'

'Don't blame him. He talked me into it. I was dead set against it, but stringing you out for all the guarantees was a great idea.'

'I'll wring his neck,' she said.

'If he takes any heat for this, it's over,' Duffy said.

'You two really have me over a barrel, don't you?'

'I'd say so.'

'What would you say if I told you I put Jim up to talking you into it?' she said.

'I'd say you were fibbing.'

'And you'd be right.'

6 Cap Duffy was breaking in a brand new unmarked squad car, and he didn't like it. 'It looks more like a police car than a patrol car does! Two whip antennas, a spotlight, blackwalled tyres, a municipal licence number. Why don't we just put a badge on the door and a flashing light on top?'

'I need to tell you something,' Jennifer said.

'I know.'

'You *know?*'

'Sure I know. You're gonna tell me that the *why* of my detective work isn't as big a reason as the note you got from Block for why you wanted to write about this investigation. That's all right.'

'How did you know *that?*'

'A detective has to be a bit of a psychologist, Mrs. Grey.'

'Jennifer.'

'Thanks, Jennifer. I mean, let's face it. No matter what you had against this guy, you've got to be curious about his death, especially after that note.'

'Even about his life, Cap.'

'Well, sure, because you never got close, right?'

'Uh-huh. And it doesn't bother you that what makes you tick is not the primary reason behind this?'

'You never said it was. It's not like you lied to me or anything.'

'But I never told you that note was the overriding reason.'

'You didn't have to, Jennifer. I knew.'

'I *will* write about you and why and how you do what you do, of course.'

'It won't make much difference to me either way.'

'Seriously? Most cops have at least a little ego, don't they?'

'Most have quite a bit of ego. I have an ego too, but it's not satisfied by seeing my name in the paper.'

'What satisfies your ego?'

'Knowing I'm doing something that few other people could do, especially shy people.'

'You really consider yourself shy?'

'Who would know better than me? I know I die inside when I have to confront people, but I play games, I playact, I overcome the barrier because I force myself. I know I have to, and so I do it, and I get great satisfaction from it.'

'And each time it gets easier?'

'It *never* gets easier. Sometimes it's more difficult. And then I use every part of my being.'

'Meaning?'

'Sometimes it's my body. I'm in the best shape of any thirty-nine-year-old you know. I can run six miles in thirty minutes, do forty pull-ups, and one hundred push-ups in two minutes. I can lift one and a half times my body weight. Detective work is not all head knowledge and fast talk. When I get into a tight spot, I have more options than most. That's where my ego boost comes from.'

'And it wouldn't give you a thrill if people knew about that?'

'It embarrasses me a little to even tell you. Nobody else but my wife knows what I go through to stay in shape. Some of the guys are aware of my condition because we play racquetball, but most of the time I hide under the clothes.'

'Tell me about the clothes.'

'Clothes are irrelevant to me. I don't know or care what most people are wearing.'

'But you dress, how should I say it — ?'

'Slovenly?'

'You said it, not me.'

'I know,' he said. 'Yeah. I do. And I'd like to be able to tell you it's for some strategic reason, but I dress the same way socially and formally. I'll tell you this, though. It works as strategy, because I'm seldom taken for a cop. Cops run the gamut from frumpy, old-fashioned outfits — trench coats, wide-brimmed hats, black shoes, and white socks — to the modern style, like off the cover of *Gentlemen's Quarterly*.'

'You can't kid me, Cap. You *do* know about fashion.'

'OK, but I still think it's basically irrelevant, except for the cover it allows me before I have to identify myself. I often get more information when I'm just hanging around someone, before they know who I am, than I do when I'm peppering them with questions.'

'Who are we going to pepper with questions this balmy Friday afternoon?'

'Don't start with the *we* business, Jennifer. I'm warning you.'

He was only half-kidding.

'Sorry,' she said. 'Who are *you* going to question?'

'I'm going back to the *Tribune*.'

'Which means *I* have to sit in the car.'

'But not for long. I've got a suspect in there who won't leave.'

'Seriously? You think it's someone Bobby worked with?'

'Slow down,' he said, pulling into an underground car-park not far from *Tribune* Tower. 'Choosing an early suspect is just one of my things. It helps me focus. I hone in, concentrate my energies, believe with everything I have that I've found the murderer, and I don't let up until I'm forced to.'

'Guilty until proved innocent, huh?'

'That's right, except — of course — I never put someone in that category without a good reason.'

'Was *I* in that category?'

'Not for a second.'

'Who's your mark at the *Trib?*'

'Name's Young. Christopher Young.'

'Chris *Young?* He used to be at the *Day!* He's a buddy of Bobby's, one of his very few. Are you sure you've got something on him?'

Duffy flashed her an impatient look. 'No, I just don't like tall, skinny guys — so I thought I'd give him some grief.'

'I'm sorry,' Jennifer said, but not quickly enough. Duffy was out of the car, slamming the door and striding toward the lift.

Chris Young? He'd got his start at the *Day*. In fact, hadn't he graduated a few years before Bobby and put in a good word for him with Leo? Chris was with the *Day* for three or four years and developed into a top-notch reporter and writer before landing a plum rewrite job at the *Trib* for excellent money.

Jennifer even vaguely remembered that it may have been Young who put the *Tribune* brass onto Bobby after Bobby had been fired from the *Day*. Chris and Bobby had been inseparable, and she had heard of no rift. But then she never heard much of anything from the *Tribune*.

What could have gone wrong in their relationship?

Duffy was back more quickly than Jennifer expected. 'Stood me up,' he said, fuming. 'That only adds fuel to the fire.'

'It doesn't necessarily mean anything,' Jennifer said.

'It means he's avoiding me, and when I've got

him in my sights, for valid reasons or not, it doesn't look good for him.'

'Tell me why his scent is in your nose.'

Duffy turned and grinned at her. 'If it ain't Ernestine Hemingway! You gonna use that line in your column about ol' Cap Duffy, the blood-hound?'

Jennifer was embarrassed. 'You know what I mean. And where are we going now?'

'Northwestern.'

Inwardly, Jennifer felt proud of herself that Duffy was sniffing around the same places she would have. As he headed north, she asked again about Chris Young.

'Ah, it's nothing big, really. Just something I sensed when we first talked. He couldn't hide his bitterness over certain injustices in Block's life.'

'Such as?'

'Such as the fact that Block was two-timing his girlfriend.'

'You mean he was dating both this Josie girl you mentioned *and* Adrienne Eden?' Jennifer asked.

'Right. Josie Sisk is a Chicagoan. Eden is still on campus at Northwestern.'

'But his buddy wouldn't kill him for that.'

'Not as a rule. Unless Young was interested in one of the young ladies.'

'Excuse me, Cap, but I don't know how to say this. The word around the *Day* was that Chris Young was more likely interested in the young men than the young ladies.'

'Yeah, I heard the gay theory about Young too. So maybe he was interested in Block and was incensed that he was losing him to not just one woman, but two.'

'Sounds pretty thin, Cap.'

'Maybe, but there's more. I got the impression that Young wanted to take a lot of credit for Block's career.'

'And he probably should. I seem to remember Chris got Bobby both his job at the *Day* and at the *Trib*.'

'Well, I got that impression too, so I probed a little deeper. I told Young that I saw Block as one of the young stars at the *Trib*, in fact in all of Chicago journalism.'

'Did that make him proud?'

'Hardly,' Duffy said. 'It opened a floodgate. Young burst forth with a lot of spiteful talk about the fact that the public should some day know the truth behind the newspaper writers in this city.'

'What did he mean — that the behind-the-scenes guys, the rewrite men, are really the writers?'

'I assume.'

'He's right, of course, Cap. *Our* rewrite men are chosen for their attitudes. That may be why Chris had to go to the *Trib* to get that kind of a position. He was too well-known at the *Day* as a hothead and a climber.'

'Not the best type for a rewrite man?'

'No way. They sit there with earphones clamped to their heads for eight hours, trying to make readable copy out of poor reporting and horrible on-the-scene writing. A guy has to have the heart of a servant and love his work — not to mention his reporters — to be a good rewrite man. You can't buy or make them — they're born.'

'In my book, Chris Young ain't one of 'em,' Duffy decided.

Jennifer nodded. 'He's got the ability. But not the psyche.'

Duffy parked on the far south side of Northwestern's campus, and they walked through the heart of the beautiful place, heading north. 'Who are we looking for — excuse me, who are *you* looking for here?'

The detective dug out his leather notebook and leafed past several pages. 'Ed McDevitt,' he said carefully. 'In his second year. On the campus newspaper staff. A protegé of the great Bobby Block. Interested in sport. Almost made the basketball team. Big in intramurals here. Tall, broad, rangy, good-lookin' kid with sandy blond hair. Real hearthrob type. Studying law. My favourite interview.'

'Law students?'

'Yeah. They'll tell ya what you're doin' right and wrong, all that. I can usually tell right away if they've got something to hide.'

'You have an appointment with this, uh — '

'McDevitt,' Duffy said, sneaking a peek at his notes. 'No, but he gets out of lectures in about fifteen minutes, and he should stroll right by here.'

They sat on a wooden bench behind a hedge and relaxed while Duffy kept an eye out for the big law student. 'We talked about your technique, Cap,' Jennifer said, 'but we still haven't got into the why.'

'Why do I do it? Why am I a cop? That type of thing?'

'Uh-huh.'

'Like most honest cops, I'm on a justice trip, I guess. Growing up I noticed that the biggest and the strongest and the best-looking and the smartest people always got the breaks, and not only that, they got away with everything. Well, I can't be put in any of those classifications, but I can be sure that justice is done.'

'But is justice always done?'

'No, 'course not. You mean because of the court system?'

Jennifer nodded.

'I hear you. We catch 'em red-handed, round 'em up, drag 'em to court. But we can't throw 'em in prison. That's up to the judge, the jury, the court, the state, and the system. And it's too big and overcrowded. That's why you see guilty people go free. And that's why you see cops tempted to carry out justice on the spot and answer questions later. Because they see something bad going down — they themselves, the cops, you understand — are the witnesses. They testify in court, they've got the culprit dead to rights, and to save time and money the judge lets the sucker cop a plea, and we've got murderers, rapists, armed robbers, you name it, on the streets with suspended or commuted sentences.'

Jennifer looked up from her own notes. 'But that's not enough to put you out of the profession?'

'Nah. If we all got discouraged with it, the whole thing would be up for grabs. A few guys get convicted, and we slow the rest down at least, make them hire lawyers and show up for court and post bond and all the rest. We make life tough for 'em anyway. There's some justice in that.'

'But not enough, I hear you saying.'

'You listen well, lady.'

They fell silent and gazed across the campus. Suddenly, Duffy stood and peered through the hedge. He pulled a couple of pictures from his pocket. 'I know that's McDevitt,' he said, 'but who's the girl?'

'Don't ask me,' Jennifer said, craning her neck to see. A dreamy giant in a heavy woollen sweater loped down the path with a sweet, little female student on his arm. At least, she looked like a student.

'Look at this picture,' Duffy said, shoving under her nose the likeness of a young woman with long, blond tresses and a short, compact body. 'Imagine her with a page-boy haircut and tell me that isn't the girl he's with.'

Jennifer compared the picture and the girl on the giant's arm. The couple neared the hedge. 'That's her,' Jennifer agreed.

'What in the world is he doing with Josie Sisk?' Duffy asked.

7 Duffy motioned to Jennifer to sit back
down on the bench. He joined her,
deftly pulling a newspaper from his
side pocket, so he would appear to have
been sitting there reading for some time when the
couple walked by.

The move made both Jennifer and Duffy blend
into the background. McDevitt and Sisk were
about thirty feet past them when Jennifer whispered, 'What now?'

'We follow them,' Duffy said, rising. Jennifer
wondered how Duffy thought he could look
inconspicuous on *this* campus.

A hundred yards away McDevitt and Sisk
stopped and leaned against the bonnet of a old
canary Porsche. Duffy sat under a tree and
Jennifer wondered what she was supposed to do.
She wasn't going to sit on the ground in her
dress.

'Just wander around,' Duffy suggested. 'If that's Josie's car, she'll be gone soon, and I'll intercept the big guy when he comes back this way.'

Jennifer was frustrated but wandered off. In a few minutes Josie Sisk pulled away, and McDevitt returned back up the pathway past Duffy. Jennifer headed that way too.

As the lanky student passed the detective, Duffy looked up from his newspaper, 'Hey,' he called, 'aren't you Ed McDevitt?'

McDevitt whirled round and glared at him, puzzled, but kept walking.

'The basketball player?' Duffy said. 'Played high school ball in, ah, don't tell me, uh — '

'Michigan,' McDevitt said, circling back. 'Do I know you?'

Duffy looked around to be sure he wasn't creating a scene that would embarrass the big guy, then pulled out his badge and identified himself. 'I want to talk to you about Bobby Block for a few minutes. Right here all right?'

'Who's the lady?' McDevitt asked, staring at Jennifer.

'She's with me,' Duffy said.

'Uh-*huh*,' McDevitt said, winking at her. She glared at him, and he smiled. She didn't. 'Let's at least sit down,' he suggested, and they found another bench. McDevitt sat in the middle. 'What do you wanna know?' he asked.

'I just need preliminary information, some help,' Duffy said.

'That's good,' McDevitt said, 'because you're out of your jurisdiction, aren't you? And if you made me sit here and talk to you without arresting me or informing me of my rights, I might have you for violating my security against unreasonable search and seizure.'

'Oh, give the kid an A on that quiz,' Duffy said with a grin. 'If it ain't Perry Mason!'

McDevitt looked annoyed.

'Hey, just kiddin',' Duffy said. 'Seriously, that was an impressive little rundown there for just a second year student in prelaw.'

'So, what else do you know about me?'

'I don't care about you, Ed. May I call you Ed? I care about your old buddy, Robert Block.'

'All of a sudden everyone cares about Bobby. I don't remember that many people caring about him when he was alive.'

'Only you?'

'A lot of the time only me. And Adrienne. I owed him.'

'For what?'

'He made time for me. He told me the odds against graduating high enough in law to get a decent job anywhere, and he said that while the journalism field has been flooded ever since Watergate and all that newspaper glamour, I had a chance if I stuck with it.'

'Stuck with *him*, you mean?'

'Well, sort of, yeah. He taught me a lot of stuff, made me less naïve. Pushed me to be tough, assertive, a digger.'

'More cynical, Ed?'

'I guess so. Especially now.'

'Why now?'

'Like I said, everyone is finally interested in a good newspaperman, now that he's gone.'

'How do you reckon he died, Ed?'

'How should I know? He had plenty of enemies. Cops didn't like him. Criminals didn't like him. Co-workers didn't like him. What can I tell you? There must be a suspect list a mile long.'

'Make that an A-plus on the quiz, kid.'

Ed McDevitt looked at his watch. 'So what do you want from me?' he asked.

Duffy looked him square in the eye. 'You really wanna know?'

McDevitt nodded carefully, as if fearing what he was getting into.

'I wanna know what you're doing holding hands and playing kissy-face with one of Block's girlfriends the day after he's found poisoned to death.'

McDevitt uncrossed his long legs and stretched them out, crossing them again at the ankles, and folding his arms across his chest. 'That make me a suspect?'

'Maybe.'

'Then arrest me and charge me. You can't do anything more or less until I'm indicted before a grand jury.'

'Oh, give me a break, Ed. You don't want me to do that any more than I do. It'd be a waste of time. I've got solid alibis on you even without your help. Just answer the question and save me a lot of grief.'

McDevitt locked into Duffy's gaze. 'All right,' he said, speaking quickly. 'You've done your homework, so I'll give you a few freebies and save you some time. First of all, Josie is *my* woman and has never been Bobby's. Bobby was engaged to Adrienne, though I don't think they ever got around to making it official with a ring. Bobby would have been a little too cheap for that.'

'You telling me Adrienne doesn't think Bobby was seeing Josie on the side?'

'Of course she thinks that, and she was right.'

'I'm not following you.'

'Bobby saw Josie, OK? It was all right with me. I owed Bobby. Whatever was mine was his.'

Jennifer couldn't contain herself. 'You've got to be kidding!' she said. McDevitt flinched and Duffy stared her down. 'Sorry,' she said, putting a finger to her own lips.

'I'm an open-minded guy,' McDevitt added. 'It didn't really bother me.'

'Baloney,' Duffy said.

'It *didn't!*'

'Baloney.'

'It wasn't a big issue.'

'Baloney.'

McDevitt appeared as if he knew Duffy had hit a weak spot. 'You won't get me to admit it was a problem for me.'

'Why?' Duffy pressed. 'Because you were so enamoured of Block that he was like a cult leader to you? Did he have you under mind control or something? I mean, what sane, healthy American in the twentieth century lets another man share his woman? Sounds a little kinky, man.'

McDevitt glared at him.

'You couldn't have liked it, Ed. You may have given in, but you couldn't have liked it.'

McDevitt said nothing.

'I'm saying it gave you a motive for murder,' Duffy added.

'But you just said you had alibis for me.'

'I do, so where am I, Ed? What've I got? Give an old detective a break.'

'You're driving at something, Duffy,' McDevitt said.

'You're right. You wanna guess?'

'Not particularly.'

'You wanna guess, ma'am?' Duffy asked Jennifer, avoiding her name.

'Sure,' she said, eliciting another double take from McDevitt. 'Ed has himself almost convinced that he didn't mind sharing his woman with Block, and he didn't want to trouble the waters for fear of losing Josie. Down deep, it troubles him greatly that she saw anything at all in a physical specimen as unimpressive as Block and that she would give any other man the time of day, let alone give him anything else. What you have, Ed, is a love-hate relationship with both Bobby *and* Josie.'

Duffy fought a grin. McDevitt looked miserable. 'Now you've got Josie all to yourself,' Duffy said, 'but you wonder how long that will last. You're hurt and disappointed, and you feel guilty because the feeling that Josie didn't care for you exclusively is stronger than the grief you feel over the loss of your friend.'

McDevitt stared at the ground.

'Do you think you know who killed Bobby?' Jennifer asked.

Ed shook his head.

'Would you have liked to?'

He nodded, grimacing.

'Were you glad to hear about it?'

His shoulders heaved, but he didn't respond. Duffy put a hand gently on his arm — surprising Jennifer — and McDevitt broke down.

'The problem,' Duffy said in the car, 'is that the man has solid alibis; he couldn't have done it. But he certainly had a motive.'

'But so did Adrienne,' Jennifer said.

'For sure. And if I can somehow eliminate Christopher Young from the list, she becomes prime.'

'I hope you can eliminate him.'

'Why? You got something in you that wants to see Adrienne Eden sentenced to death? I thought you hardly knew the woman.'

'That's not it at all, Cap. Good grief, I don't want to see anyone die, though I share your interest in justice, especially in a murder case.'

'You're one of those liberal left-wing news types that doesn't believe in capital punishment though, right?'

'If you've read my column for any length of time, you'd know how wrong you are about that.'

'So why are you so eager to see Christopher Young cleared?'

'Because I don't know what I'd do with it in my column if a member of a competing paper's staff was a murderer.'

Shocking Jennifer, Cap Duffy suddenly braked and pulled off to the shoulder of the road. He shifted into park and let the engine idle. With both hands gripping the wheel he turned to face her.

'I've finally found the chink,' he said.

'The chink?'

'The chink in your armour. I knew you were too good to be true.'

'What are you saying, Cap? Or should I ask, what did *I* say?'

'You just showed your true colours, that's all. Are you saying that your management wouldn't let you cover it in your paper if a competitor was guilty and that they would expect the same courtesy?'

'No, I'm saying *I* personally would have a problem with it. I wouldn't want to cover it, to deal with it, to write about it.'

Duffy shook his head slowly and pulled back out into traffic.

'You're disappointed in me,' Jennifer said. 'I can see it all over your face.'

'I guess I'm just a little surprised, that's all. I was kinda hoping — '

'Hoping what?'

'That you were different, like you seemed.'

'That hurts. I'd like to think I'm different from most people in many ways.'

'But not when it comes to fairness and objectivity.'

He waited for a response, but she couldn't speak.

'What would you want me to do,' he said, 'if I

found out the murderer was a cop? Sweep it under the rug? I've read your columns about *that*, haven't I? I applauded your stand on that, tough as it was. You called for consistency and firmness, quick and decisive justice. Cops were beneficiaries of the public trust, you said.'

'You *do* read my column,' she said wondering how he could remember her exact words.

'I read the ones that apply to me. You wanna know if I'm disappointed — yeah, I'm disappointed. I've got a columnist riding around with me, wanting to write about me and what I do. But what you'll write is gonna hinge on just who the murderer is and what walk of life he hails from, not whether or how we catch him — or her.'

'I never said that, Cap.'

'You did!'

'I didn't mean that.'

'Just what did you mean when you said you wouldn't be able to handle writing about a murderer who was from your profession, a competitor from another local paper?'

'Well, I didn't mean I actually wouldn't do it.'

'But that's what you said.'

'It is, isn't it? I'm sorry, because I know better.'

'I hope so.'

'I do.'

'I wonder,' Cap said.

'Don't say that. You couldn't hurt me more.'

He looked at her with a puzzled look. 'You're serious?'

She nodded, almost in tears.

'I really hoped your integrity meant that much to you,' he said.

'Tomorrow I'll talk to Adrienne Eden and Christopher Young,' Duffy said, parking behind the *Day* building.

'In other words, I won't be in on either of those.'

'Probably not,' Duffy said. 'But you'll be close by, and I'll fill you in.'

As Jennifer was opening her door and thanking him for putting up with her for the afternoon, a message crackled over the radio that he should telephone the station. 'Ten-four' he said.

Few of the daytime staff were still in the office, so Jennifer let Duffy use Stephanie's phone, then checked her own desk for messages and tidied up her office.

Duffy appeared in the doorway, ashen faced. 'You tired?' he asked.

It was a strange question, she decided. 'Why?'

'We've got a big night ahead of us, if you're up to it.'

Jennifer was baffled. 'Well, what's happening, Cap? I'm supposed to meet Jim in about an hour, but if — '

'I'm on my way back to Evanston,' he said. 'Adrienne Eden was found by her roommate.'

'She was found?'

'Dead.'

8 As they sped north again, Jennifer told Cap Duffy that she was surprised to see him so affected by someone's death. 'I would think you'd get used to murder after a while.'

'There are days,' he admitted, 'when the bodies and crime scenes seem like nothing more than grist for the puzzle mill. On those days, it's just a job. Interesting, but just a task. But it always hits me hard when the victim is someone I've already talked to or someone who's a key to the investigation, as in this case.'

Jennifer asked if Adrienne Eden had been a key in the investigation for any other reason than the fact that she knew Bobby was seeing Josie on the side.

'That, and the fact that she had a key to his apartment. A murderer needs motive, means, and opportunity. She had the first and the last.

I'm not sure how poison injected into the system would be characteristic of her. She was a communications student, not a biologist.'

The radio came alive again, informing Duffy that two eyewitnesses had placed the female in photograph number 08653 in the Block apartment building as late as midnight Wednesday night. Duffy reached into his breast pocket and tossed his whole packet of photographs to Jennifer.

She thumbed through them, pausing at the grisly autopsy photos of Bobby Block. There was McDevitt, Eden, Young, Sisk, and even herself. 'The numbers are on the back,' Duffy said. 'See if Eden is the number he just read off.'

'What was the number?'

'Zero-eight-six-five-three.'

'How do you remember that?'

'The zero is easy. I pretended it was ten and the rest went down, two evens and two odds, in order.'

'Incredible. Nope. That's not Eden's number.'

'Is it yours? It better not be — or you and a lot of your friends lied to me.'

Jennifer nearly panicked as she flipped her photo over. 'Nope, not me either,' she said.

'Sisk,' he said. She turned over Josie's photo.

'Right,' she said quietly.

'Do you realize,' he said, 'that the woman has had a drastic haircut since Thursday night?'

'And two people place her at the scene of the crime that night?'

'Yup.'

'Can I ask you something a little off the subject? Have you been involved in enough autopsies to know how much weight a body should lose during one?'

'Yeah. A body can lose a lot of fluid, but if you're asking about those pictures of Block, they were taken before the autopsy, so he wouldn't have lost much weight there. Why?'

'I must not have been keeping up with him at all. His face seems a lot thinner than the way I remember him.'

'Well, he was still a big boy there. I'd guess about sixteen stone.'

'But when he was at the *Day* he weighed more than eighteen. When I saw him just a couple of months ago, he was as big as ever, so he would have had to have lost all that weight pretty quickly.'

'Interesting,' Duffy said, 'because you know what we found, or I should say, what we didn't find?'

'Hm?'

'Evidence that he had eaten any of that breakfast on his table Thursday morning. It was as if he had made it for someone else and was waiting for them.'

'Any evidence of Josie Sisk in the place?' Jennifer asked.

'Some unidentified fingerprints that we can perhaps trace to her. She shouldn't be hard to find.'

'Have you matched the prints against Adrienne?'

'No, but that won't be too difficult now either, will it?'

Jennifer just stared at Duffy. 'If she was murdered by the same *modus operandi*, she's no longer a suspect, is she?'

'As a rule, that's true,' Duffy said.

'Who are you leaning toward now, Cap?' Jennifer asked, reorganizing the photos and returning them to him so she could take notes.

'Let's just say I'll be very interested to know if Christopher Young or Josie Sisk were seen in the vicinity of Adrienne's room during the last twenty-four hours.'

'How will you find out?'

'There are no shortcuts to that,' the detective said. 'You just keep knocking on doors, asking questions, showing pictures, and hoping someone will have a good combination of memory and honesty. The honest ones usually can't remember, and the ones who remember will say they don't.'

When Duffy and Jennifer arrived at the Northwestern security command post, campus guards and Evanston detectives were talking to Adrienne Eden's roommate, Lisa Johnson, a tiny girl with curly, dark brown hair and huge, square-lensed glasses. 'I only shared with her since January, and I learned to hate her with a passion, but this is horrible! She was lying face down at the door when I came back from dinner at five o'clock. She was a terrible person, but I wouldn't have killed her!'

Jennifer followed Duffy to the apartment, where the scene reminded her of Thursday afternoon at Bobby Block's. Jake Steinmetz would not cover this one himself, it being so far north, but Duffy quickly located a coroner's assistant.

'You wouldn't wanna help me with a little pre-autopsy, would you?' he asked.

The doctor glared at him. 'You can't touch that body.'

'I know,' Duffy said, showing his badge. 'I just need to know if there are any puncture wounds just below the right hip. It'll aid in the investigation, and I really can't wait until tomorrow.'

The doctor pursed his lips and stared, then reached into his bag for a penlight. He draped a sheet over the fully clothed body and moved everyone else from the immediate area. Within minutes, he returned. 'Bingo,' he said. 'About an inch square, maybe ten tiny puncture holes, none of them terribly recent.'

'How recent?'

'The freshest could have been twenty-four hours ago.'

Jennifer pulled Duffy aside. 'What's going on?' she said. 'Adrienne seems to have dropped a lot of weight fast too. When I saw her at Bobby's place, she was wearing a baggy top and I didn't notice, but she's lost maybe twenty pounds. What do you make of it?'

'They were both on diets? I don't know, Jennifer. What do *you* make of it?'

She shrugged. 'I'd like to ask the roommate about it.'

'I'd better,' he said.

When they arrived back at the security office, Lisa Johnson was begging for somewhere else to stay. 'I don't even want to go in there to get my things with a murderer on the loose. You've got to help me move! How am I supposed to concentrate on my studies?'

Duffy received permission to question her briefly. He asked about her roommate's weight loss.

'Yeah, it's just been over the last several weeks. I don't know. We never have meals together anyway, but she hasn't eaten a thing between meals like she used to. She never talked about it. She just stopped eating snacks. She smoked a lot of grass, though. I thought maybe she got on to some harder stuff and lost her appetite, but I never saw anything around the place.'

'How about you?' Duffy said.

'How about me?'

'You take any drugs?'

'Just a little grass, a long time ago.'

'Nothing harder?'

'Cocaine. Once. Nearly scared me to death.'

'Never dropped acid?'

'Never. What do you want from me?'

'Nothing. Thank you.'

'I can go?'

'That's up to these gentlemen.'

Jennifer and Duffy spent the rest of the evening, until quite late, questioning everyone within a quarter mile radius of the Eden-Johnson room.

Duffy was right. Most people were hostile, not wanting to talk when they found out what had happened. Others were just curious and asked more questions than they answered. Everyone knew Ed McDevitt, but no one had seen him around that area recently.

Everyone knew the Porsche that apparently belonged to his girlfriend, but no one had seen that around lately either.

The first break came just after Jennifer had called Jim to change their plans for the evening. He volunteered to come and help in the canvassing, but Duffy felt it unnecessary.

A senior girl, living alone on the top floor of Adrienne's building, had seen Christopher Young in the library earlier in the day. 'It was about four o'clock, and he was talking with a tall, good-looking guy in a sweater, the guy who usually drives around in a yellow Porsche.'

Had she seen either of them later? 'No.'

Had she seen the car that day? 'Yes, right here at this building when I returned from the library. That's what struck me as strange, because I had seen the driver somewhere else.'

'Who was driving the car when you saw it?' Duffy wanted to know.

'I didn't see anyone in the car, but I passed a girl on the stairs, and the next time I looked out, the car was gone.'

'Is this the girl?' Duffy asked, showing the photo of Josie Sisk.

'That's her,' the student said. 'But that's not her hair. Either that's a wig, or she's had it cut since that picture was taken.'

Duffy got the girl to agree to swear to what she had said, in court if necessary. Two others on the same floor corroborated much of her story. Duffy was elated.

'You think Josie could be your murderer?' Jennifer asked.

'I think we've got enough to warrant picking her up and fingerprinting her, don't you?'

Jennifer nodded.

'And if her prints match those found in Block's apartment?'

'Then I'd say the girl is in serious trouble.'

The Chicago and Evanston police put out all points bulletins for Josie Sisk. When Duffy and Jennifer reached the city again, a message was waiting for Duffy to call Dr. Steinmetz.

'He's going to tell me that they found a similar patch of injection marks on the second body,' he predicted.

He was wrong.

'I know you know all of that, Cap,' Jake said. 'I'm surprised you didn't ask for a full autopsy right there in the room. There's nothing too surprising to report, but there are two new developments, one of which I can tell you by phone, and the other I'd like to share with you in person.'

'I wish you could tell me both by phone, Jake,' Duffy said. 'I'm about ready to drop.'

'Sorry. I'll give you the first half now and the second whenever you say, but not by phone.'

'OK, shoot,'

'I don't know what this means. You can put it into the hopper and see what comes of it. But we found traces of an appetite suppressant in the tissues of both bodies.'

'That significant?'

'You tell me. Could mean that both were on

diets, but this suppressant is not available over-the-counter. It's usually administered only by injection, by a doctor.'

'Would that account for the needle marks?'

'Probably.'

'Could the suppressant be lethal?'

'Only in mega-doses, and it would not cause the types of deaths we saw here. Both of these young adults died on what appears to be a timed release basis. If it hadn't happened twice, and if I weren't always hanging around you suspicious homicide types, I'd probably guess that someone blew the injection, gave the patient something other than what he was supposed to. But two? And people who knew each other? And no similar deaths reported? Too coincidental.'

'You wanna swop jobs?' Duffy gibed.

'Over my dead bodies,' the coroner said.

'Listen, Jake, do I really hafta wait until we can get together on your other titbit?'

'Afraid so, Cap. I'm sorry. I'm not even sure it's any more significant than what I just gave you, but it just seems important to me to keep it for other than a phone conversation. Indulge me.'

'Fair enough, if you'll indulge me.'

'Anything.'

'I want to bring Jennifer Grey along when you tell me.'

'You can bring her around any time. But seriously, Cap, you'd better get her to agree in advance that she won't print this information unless you or I give her the go-ahead, and even that will hinge on the wishes of the next of kin.'

'The next of kin?'

'You heard me.'

'You're gonna make me come out to see you tonight, aren't you?'

'No, I wouldn't do that. Really, Cap, it'll wait till morning, and we can meet in my office.'

'You're going to be in on a Saturday morning?'

'You're working tomorrow, aren't you, Cap?'

'Well, yeah, but — '

'Well, I'm just as eager to see this thing solved as you are.'

Jennifer slept fitfully, in spite of her exhaustion, and she wondered how a mind like Duffy's ever rested. She bet if she called him he'd be up pacing, making notes. But she didn't dare.

Jennifer's mind wandered, raced, slowed, slept, awoke, and thought some more. Did she have to decide between Chris Young, whom she hadn't seen for ages, and Josie Sisk, whom she'd never spoken to? Why would either of them murder both Bobby *and* Adrienne? It didn't make sense. And what was Chris doing talking to Ed after Ed had talked with Cap? Chris had stood up Cap.

At 3:00 a.m. the phone rang, and Jennifer didn't recognize it at first. *Why is that alarm so loud? Is it really six forty-five already?* When she realized it was the phone, it scared her. She didn't like surprise phone calls.

Could something have happened to Jim?

'Hello?'

'Jennifer?'

'Jim?'

'No.'

'Who's calling please?'

'Don't you recognize my voice? It's an old friend.'

'Who's calling please? It's three o'clock in the morning.'

'I know, and I'm sorry to bother you, Jennifer. But I have some information that might help you and your detective friend. Can I meet with you without him there?'

'Chris?'

'Yes. Can I?'

'Where?'

'Lincoln Park, tomorrow morning.'

'Make it noon and you've got a deal.'

'Noon then. But come alone.'

9 For the sake of her sanity, Jennifer called Jim and met him for breakfast. She told him everything. Well, almost everything. Everything except the scheduled meeting with Christopher Young.

'What could the coroner possibly have up his sleeve?' she wondered aloud.

'Embalming fluid?' Jim tried.

Jennifer choked. 'You're as morbid as he is. You should have heard what he said to Duffy last night.'

'You already told me.'

Jennifer rested her head in her hands. 'I'm sorry. I'm just exhausted. But think of Duffy.'

'I'd rather think of you, but, yeah, I know the homicide guys put in some long hours. You can't schedule when the breaks will fall into your lap.'

'I get the impression that Duffy makes more breaks than he waits for, though,' she said.

'Impressive, huh? Didn't I tell you?'

'You didn't tell me half of what I've discovered in Cap Duffy. Really quite a character.'

'I like him,' Jim said.

'I'm not sure whether I like him yet,' Jennifer said. 'But he *is* interesting. I've already got a couple of columns rattling around in my head, and we've hardly started the investigation.'

'Sounds like it's almost over, Jenn. If you can tie Young with Sisk somehow, you've got conspiracy, collusion, whatever you want. And if you can't tie 'em together, one is probably guilty.'

'I don't know, Jim. It almost sounds too easy.'

'Then make it hard, Jenn. It'll make for a better column.'

'Eat your breakfast.'

Cap Duffy was stony when Jennifer met him in the downstairs lobby of the building that housed the medical examiner's office. 'You wanna talk about it,' Jennifer said, 'or are you just not a morning person?'

'I'm enough of a morning person,' he said. 'It's just that very few of the prints we pulled in Block's apartment match with the Eden girl, but plenty of 'em match Sisk.'

'That should make you happy. Where'd you find Sisk?'

'That's just it. We didn't. She's gone. McDevitt isn't talking, and I tend to believe he really doesn't know where she is.'

'Why is he so believable all of a sudden?'

'Because he gave us several leads on where we

might find her. All dead ends so far, but I think he's really trying.'

'If she's got his car, she'll be easy to track.'

'She hasn't,' Duffy said.

'How'd you get the prints if you don't have her?'

'We got a warrant and pulled a set from her apartment, which, by the way, is not too far from Block's. Then we got an old set from the state police. She was kind of a rowdy in high school and got busted a couple times when she was eighteen. Just old enough to make 'em keep her prints on file.'

As they sat in Dr. Steinmetz's stylish waiting room, Duffy continued. 'We also got Sisk's prints from Adrienne's place.'

'Doesn't that just about wrap it up, Cap?'

'You'd think so, but it's all circumstantial. Pretty impressive circumstances, I would say, with eyewitnesses placing her at the scenes of the deaths. Notice I didn't say she was placed at the scenes of the *crimes*.'

'What's your point?'

'Just that I'm not sure the places where we found Block and Eden dead were the places where the crimes were perpetrated. There's little evidence that Josie was at either place when the victims actually died.'

'I can see why you're frustrated.'

'That's not all of it. I'm also upset with this crazy Young character. I've got a much better suspect, yet Young chooses to run now. I tried to reach him at his office this morning, and he's on some three-day leave of absence. No one is saying where he went. If he's innocent, what's he running from?'

'Maybe he's involved in the thing with Sisk,' Jennifer said.

Duffy apparently didn't want to waste time thinking about it. 'Yeah, well, who knows?' he said. 'He'd do himself a big favour by sticking around long enough to get cleared.'

'If he's innocent, you mean.'

Duffy cocked his head and pointed at Jennifer, as if conceding the point. Then they were called into Dr. Steinmetz's office, a beautiful, book-lined, mahogany sanctuary.

'It ain't much, but it's comfortable,' Jake dead-panned.

'Yeah,' Duffy added, 'and paid for.'

'That it's not,' Steinmetz admitted. 'Sit down, please.'

They sat at a small antique table near a leather sofa. The coroner had the Block file on the table, secured by two large rubber bands he never removed, though he frequently tugged at them and let them slap the manila folder.

'Did you inform Miss Grey that this is off-the-record until we say it isn't?'

Duffy nodded, and they both looked to Jennifer. 'If you say it's off-the-record gentlemen, it's off-the-record. I *do* hope you'll cut off the restraint as soon as possible though, whatever the information is.'

Steinmetz scowled and stared at his hands, then rose and slowly paced the room, stopping at the ten-foot window casing where he pulled back a heavy, dark curtain and peered out into brilliant sunlight. When he let go of the curtain, the room returned to a yellow dullness, illuminated by just two table lamps.

'Well, Cap,' Jake said, turning to face him with his hands in his pockets pushing his charcoal three-piece jacket back, 'as I said, I'm not sure of the significance of this, but here goes.

'Remember I told you that a couple of pathologists and I were doing some further work on the Block body the other night?'

Duffy nodded.

'We found something we didn't expect. We found something we couldn't have seen before because we weren't looking for it, and even if we had been, we were looking in the wrong place. The boy had colon cancer, Cap, and I would have given him fewer than six months to live.'

Silence hung in the room for several minutes. Finally, Jennifer asked, 'How long would he have had it?'

'Could have been a couple of years. It would have had the symptoms of colonitis at first and would have been terribly painful and depressing. The cancer then can be held in check for some time. But once it kicks up again after a brief remission, it's only a matter of time.

'My colleagues agree he was in the last stages of life. It was an ugly mess that would have killed him, even if it hadn't spread too far, which — we discovered — it had.'

'Shouldn't you have been able to see that right away?' Cap asked.

'Another medical examiner might have. Then

again, there was no reason to examine the colon the first time through. We found what we felt had killed him, and we saved the more careful work for later.'

'Are you saying the cancer killed him?' Jennifer said.

'No, no, not at all. Don't misunderstand that. He still had several months, and he had to have known about it. But it was an as yet undetermined poison that shut down his cardiovascular and respiratory systems.'

Duffy sat thinking, jotting a few notes in his neat script. No one spoke until he said, just above a whisper, 'You wonder if we're looking at a suicide here, don't you, Jake?'

The doctor gave a wan smile. 'That's not my department, Cap.'

'Sure it is. You're supposed to speculate about the cause of death.'

'I can tell you *what* did it, Cap. But when I list "person or persons unknown", I mean it. The person could have been Robert Block, but I don't know. I just don't know.'

'Suicide crossed your mind?' Jennifer asked.

'I'll admit that.'

'How about a double suicide?' Cap suggested, startling Jennifer.

'I thought of that too,' Steinmetz said sadly. 'He knew, she knew. His death was the trigger. She followed suit. It's possible.'

'Yeah, it's possible,' Duffy said. 'But there are too many other people involved, and too few of them are in the clear yet. I'm still in the chase.'

'And well you should be,' Jake said. 'I just thought you should know.'

'I appreciate it, Doc. You know that.'

Jennifer fought tears. 'I appreciate it too, Jake.'

'But you won't print it.'

'No, of course not. Some day, maybe. To me its vindication for Bobby in a way.'

'You mean if it was a suicide.'

'No, even if it wasn't. It explains him, his temperament, his attitude. It doesn't justify anything. Many people become courageous heroes in their final days, but at least it explains a few things. People, many people, should know that.'

'But not now.'

'Whenever you say,' Jennifer said.

Neither Duffy nor Jennifer spoke as they took the lift to the ground floor and trudged to the car. In fact, they had ridden around the city for twenty minutes before Jennifer finally asked where they were going. Cap admitted that he hadn't the foggiest idea.

'You got a column to write or anything?'

'Sure, but I don't want to miss anything.'

'You won't,' he said. 'I'm just going back over all my notes and try to piece together the last full day of both victims' lives. I really can't do much now until I find Young or the APB turns up Josie Sisk. And when was the last time you heard of an all points bulletin working as fast as you'd like?'

'Could I watch you recreate the last days by going through your notes?' Jennifer asked.

'I'd really rather you not. It's kind of a silent

process, and having to talk my way through it would ruin my concentration. If you don't mind.'

'I don't mind,' she said, feeling guilty about not telling him about Chris Young. 'I should be back at the office by eleven-thirty anyway to make a noon appointment.'

'You want me to call you if we turn up Sisk?'

'Sure.'

'You can break your appointment if necessary?'

'Well, no, if you find her around noon, I'll just have to catch up with you later.'

'You've got an hour,' Duffy said. 'You wanna get some coffee?'

For some reason, that sounded great to Jennifer. It would take her mind off Bobby's disease and her secret meeting at noon.

In a vinyl and linoleum designed coffee shop at the corner of Clark and Chicago, Jennifer asked Cap if she could ask him something totally unrelated to the case — sort of personal — and would he promise not to be offended or afraid to tell her to mind her own business.

'I'm already dying of curiosity,' he said. 'Fire away.'

'Well, it's just that when we first met, you mentioned that you had been to holiday Bible school as a child.'

'Yeah.'

'I'm curious about that.'

'Oh, it's just a thing that churches have and they invite all the kids from the neighbourhood, whether they go to that church or not. I didn't go to the church. In fact, we didn't go to any church except some ethnic orthodox thing at Easter and Christmas. I don't even remember the name of that, but it was huge and frightening.'

'You talked about holiday Bible school as if you still remembered a lot of it. Did you go every year?'

'No, I only went once. It was a week or so long, and we had fun.' For a moment Cap stared out the window at the traffic on Clark Street, but his eyes were unfocused. His speech slowed. He was a child of nine, running up the street to holiday Bible school.

'We made stuff,' he said. 'And there was this guy, Uncle Chuck he called himself. I never saw him before or since, though he called at the house a few times. My father wouldn't let him see me. He said the church had me for a week and almost ruined me for life, and that was all he was going to stand for.'

'How did it almost ruin your life?'

'Oh, it didn't really. My dad was just scared. Afraid of the unknown. See, one day I came home saved, and it just about did him in.'

'Saved?' Jennifer said, knowing exactly what Cap was talking about but wondering if *he* did.

'Yeah, saved. I was singing all the songs about having met Jesus at the crossroads and choosing to follow Him. I *had* chosen to follow Him too, and I mean I meant it. It was real. Isn't that funny?'

'I don't think it's funny at all, Cap.'

'Well, ya know, I didn't either. I was devout for a kid who wasn't allowed to go back to where all the fun and the treats and the kids and the games and the stories were. I kept some of the papers and booklets and stuff and read them until they wore out. I still remember the verses, like the one that came back to me the other day. And I remember the Bible stories too.'

'But you never went back to church?'

'Not until I was in the army. I tried a few churches that didn't appeal to me. And when we got married, my wife and I went to the same kind of church that she grew up in. But we just kind of faded away from it. You know, it's a funny thing —'

'What, Cap?'

'I'm glad you asked about that because I don't think I've ever in my whole life told anyone except my mum and dad about being saved. Not even my wife.'

'That's sad.'

'Yeah, it kinda is, because it was such a shaping experience for me.'

'In what way?'

'I don't know. It made me a different person, it really did. For a long time I prayed to Jesus every day, asking Him what I should do or not do.'

'And did He tell you?'

'Well, my conscience worked overtime. You know, I grew up in a pretty rough ethnic neighbourhood. But after that, I never once got into serious trouble. I never stole anything again, I stopped beating up kids, I never skipped school — that was unheard of — and I never smoked or drank. Well, I tried it a couple of times and didn't like it — so I never did it, not even in the services. And, you know, I never was unfaithful to my wife, even before we were married — you know what I mean.'

Jennifer nodded. 'And you credit that to this experience you had as a child?'

'Oh, I'm sure of it. I wasn't raised by any example of virtue, though my mother was a pretty decent woman. But you know, to this day I don't even lie. I've never cheated on my income tax. I don't take advantage of other people's mistakes that go in my favour.'

'All because you were saved?'

'Well, why else?'

'You still pray?'

'No, not really.'

'You still believe there's a God who loves you and a Jesus who saved you from your sins?'

'Sort of, yeah, I do. I know that sounds crazy, but there's no logical reason for the basically honest type of person I am. The odds all pointed in the other direction, but something happened to me in holiday Bible school when Uncle Chuck prayed with me.'

'Can we talk more about this sometime, Cap?'

'Sure, if you want to. But I don't want any of this in the paper, Jennifer. You understand? None of it. All of this was off-the-record.'

10 Jennifer cruised around Lincoln Park until she spotted Chris Young. He was leaning against the front door of his light blue, four-door, Ford near a viaduct. His arms were folded across his chest, and his feet were crossed at the ankles. He wore sunglasses and stood so still he could have been asleep.

Jennifer pulled up next to him and wound down her window, but she said nothing. Because of his dark glasses, she couldn't tell if he saw her yet. She was tempted to honk the horn, but she didn't. She just sat there with the engine running.

Finally he grinned a tight-lipped smile and uncrossed his arms and legs. He put both hands on top of her car and leaned from the waist to put his face next to hers. 'Wanna go for a ride?' he asked.

'Not in your car,' she said, amazing herself at her calmness.

'You don't trust me?'

'Should I?'

'What, that detective buddy of yours been filling your pretty little head with stories about the homicidal homosexual?'

'No, but I don't understand why you're avoiding him if you're innocent.'

'I just don't need the hassle, Jennifer. Anyway, I wanted to give *you* my information, not him.'

'What information?'

'My car or yours?' he asked.

'Not yours.'

'You still don't trust me, and I'm doing you this favour?'

She didn't respond.

'All right then, I'll ride with you.' He loped around to the other side of his car and pulled a brown paper-wrapped package from the glove compartment, secured with masking tape. Jennifer tried not to let her imagination run wild and decided she wouldn't ask about the package.

He slid into the passenger's seat and smiled at her. She did not intend to be pleasant. 'Will you take off those ridiculous glasses?' she asked. 'It's overcast, for pete's sake!'

He looked disgusted with her but took them off and jammed them into his shirt pocket, pouting. 'So where am I supposed to go?' she said.

'Anywhere. Just go up on the Drive, and you can pull off into one of the beach parking areas.'

'You'll forgive me if I keep us in plain sight of the Drive.'

He shook his head. 'You really *are* paranoid, aren't you?'

'Shouldn't I be? Two people have been murdered in apparently bizarre ways, and you and I knew both of them. How do I know you're not going to drag me off somewhere and stick me with a needle and leave me gasping for breath?'

'How do *I* know *you* won't do the same to me? You had more of a motive for killing Bobby than I did.'

'*You* afraid of *me?*' she said to the towering Young. 'That'll be the day.' She pulled off Lake Shore Drive into a parking area. 'Now, let's get on with this.'

'You in a hurry?'

Jennifer wanted to say yes, because no one knew where she was. But she decided that was just the kind of information Chris shouldn't have.

'I *will* be expected back soon,' she said, knowing that at least her boss would wonder where she was.

'Let's take a quick walk, then.'

'I'm not taking any quick walk, Chris! Tell me whatever you're going to tell me or give me whatever you're going to give me and let me get out of here, OK?'

'OK!' he said, swearing. He shook his head again and turned away from her to stare out the window. 'I've got something for you, but I've gotta be like Deep Throat in the Watergate thing.'

'You've got to what?' she said, incredulously.

'I've got to remain anonymous. You can't write in your column where you got this stuff. I mean, it'll be obvious you got it from an insider, and you may want to say it was someone from the *Tribune* so people won't think it was from Josie.'

'I'll at least be telling Duffy and Jim Purcell,' she said.

'No! You can't! Then it's no deal!'

'What's the matter, Chris? You think I'm going to let Cap Duffy waste his time looking for you when there's no need? I'm already going to get a lot of flak for not telling him I was coming to see you.'

Young stared at her. 'You *really* didn't tell him? I can hardly believe that.'

Jennifer could have kicked herself. What she didn't need was to make herself more vulnerable to this character. 'No, I didn't. But I'm going to, and you can't stop me.'

'Then maybe I won't give you what I was going to give you.'

'Suit yourself, Chris,' she said. 'I'm tired of this game.'

'I thought you were a curious reporter-columnist,' he tried.

'I am. I'm curious to know if I'm going to survive this crazy meeting.'

It was obvious he got great delight in imagining that she was really afraid of him. He could barely contain a smile. 'You're really worried, aren't you?'

'Yes, I am. But let me tell you something, Chris. Unless you're armed, you're going to regret it if you try anything with me.'

'Oh, excuse me, lady! I'm really scared now!

What are you going to do — hit me with your bag?'

'I'm not saying I could defend myself for long, Chris, and you may wind up killing me, but I guarantee you'll regret it.'

Young opened his door and staggered from the car, laughing hysterically and banging on the bonnet. 'You're too good!' he shouted gleefully. 'You're too funny!'

He had left his package on the seat between them, and when he turned his back to howl into the wind, Jennifer swept it to the floor and beneath her seat. She jumped from the car and smiled at him. 'I guess I have been a little silly,' she said. 'I really don't think you're the murderer, Chris, and I know you wouldn't try to hurt me.'

He was still laughing. 'Really, Jennifer, what were you going to do to me? When you were really worried about me, I mean?'

She didn't appreciate being laughed at. She reached into her bag and pulled out her key ring, letting a tiny sheath of metal protrude between the ring and middle fingers of her right hand. 'I would have used this,' she said snapping her wrist and causing the metal to pivot away on its hinge and exposing a two-inch, razor-sharp blade.

Young flinched and stepped back, suddenly sober. 'You would have seriously used that on me?' he said.

'If necessary. Of course.'

'Well, I don't have, nor did I ever have, any plans to harm you, Jennifer. You should know that.'

'Don't make my caution *my* problem, Chris. You're the murder suspect who's eluding the police, not me. I don't think it's so weird for me to be prepared to protect myself.'

'So, you trust me enough now to take a little walk?'

'I don't trust you much, but I guess we can walk. Not far though. Not out of sight of the Drive.'

As they walked through a small row of trees, he said, 'I just want to give you something that belonged to Bobby. But first you have to promise that you won't tell anyone that you got it from me or that you even saw me.'

Jennifer just kept walking, her head down, yet always aware of her proximity to Lake Shore Drive, the car, and Chris. When they were about 150 feet from the car, she stopped and looked up at him. 'I already told you, I have to tell at least two people that I saw you. I —'

He interrupted with a string of profanities that sent her stomping back toward the car.

He hurried along beside her, berating her, begging her, trying to reason with her. 'I can't give you his stuff unless you promise, Jennifer. I haven't even read it, haven't even *opened* it, so I don't know or care what's in there. I just had a hunch it might help in the investigation, that's all!'

'What do you care about the investigation?' she asked. 'You won't even talk to Duffy.'

'All right, that's it!' Young said. 'Forget it! You're gonna tell him you saw me, but I'll be long gone when he comes looking for me, and I'll burn what I was going to give you!'

'Do whatever you have to do, Chris,' Jennifer said.

He hurried ahead of her to the car and opened the passenger door. She prayed he wouldn't look under the seat. He backed out of the car and wailed. 'Jennifer! We left the car unlocked! Now where's my package? Someone's stolen it! Jennifer!'

She tried to look concerned and hurried to him. 'Where was it?' she asked.

'Right there on the seat!' he said, nearly in tears. 'Jennifer, you tricked me! Someone's here! Someone's been watching us! You took the walk so someone could steal my package from the car!'

'How would they know you were going to leave anything in the car, Chris? Don't be ridiculous; there's no one here.'

He lunged at her and grabbed her by both lapels, pulling her face up to his. His eyes were wild, and he grimaced as he spoke. 'I've got to find that package,' he hissed. 'Even thinking of giving it to you was a betrayal of my dead friend. It was private! And if you tell *anyone* you saw me, you'll never get it.' He began to cry. 'Oh, Jennifer, I have to get it back! And you have to promise you won't tell anyone, so I can give it to you.'

'Forget it,' she said.

His hands slid up to her collar and his palms went to her neck, thumbs in front. She drove her right hand between his arms in an uppercut and stopped with the tip of her small blade resting lightly under his chin. He slowly released his grip on her neck and raised both hands, palms open, fear in his eyes.

She kept the blade under his chin with her right hand and gently guided him back, her left hand slipping a small chemical spray cannister from her pocket. She gave him a miniscule blast of mist in the face and pulled the blade away as he tripped backward over a carstop and sprawled in the gravel at the edge of the parking area.

She turned and ran to her car, calling over her shoulder, 'You can walk back to Lincoln Park!'

As she pulled away he scrambled to his feet and chased the car. He got close enough to bang both fists on the boot before he fell face first to the ground. He made a sickening sight in her rear-view mirror, a tall, skinny, miserable excuse for an adult, lying face down, sobbing, and slamming his fists on the ground.

Jennifer was shaking as she parked behind the *Day* building and reached beneath the seat. For several minutes, she worked at the masking tape on the package until she ruefully realized that the weapon she had so deftly used on Chris Young would also work on his package. It sliced open easily.

Inside she found twelve thin, neatly and alternately stacked reporter's spiral notebooks, the type that fit easily into a suit coat side pocket. Each was marked 'Private and Confidential' and bore a sticker that said, 'If found, please call Robert Block at the *Chicago Tribune* immediately. Reward.'

Each was also dated, and a quick leaf through

the first notebook, the one that began January 1, showed that Block had learned how to best use the reporter's most valuable tool. Each entry was dated and timed. The interview notes and miscellaneous information had been scribbled almost illegibly, but having worked with him, Jennifer was able to decipher it. Since such information had been ruled admissible in court — in the Watergate hearings — young reporters like Block had learned to protect themselves with meticulous records and direct quotes and research information.

It was a gold mine, Jennifer knew. From the boot she grabbed the briefcase she seldom used, carefully placed the rewrapped package inside, and locked the latches. When she got to her office, the Saturday secretary, Gail, was waiting with a message for Jennifer to call Duffy at the Chicago Avenue station.

'You wanna talk by phone, or shall I come over there?' Jennifer asked when she reached him. 'I've got some exciting stuff for you.'

'Likewise,' he said. 'We've found both Sisk and Young.'

'Are you serious?' she asked.

''Course. Sisk wasn't far away and wound up turning herself in. Young was found wandering down Lake Shore Drive, crying and claiming he'd been the victim of a hit and run driver near the beach. What've you got for me?'

Jennifer was laughing so hard she couldn't speak. As she hung up she called out, 'Gail! Please call Duffy back and ask him to call me when he's released Young. I'll go and see him then.'

11

'Young is a first-class weirdo,' Duffy told Jennifer just after three o'clock. 'His eyes were bloodshot, and he couldn't stop crying. I still say he had a motive, but his alibis have all checked out since I last talked to him. We had to let him go. I have this nagging suspicion that he knows more than he's letting on, and he keeps saying cryptic things about what you should know.'

'What *I* should know?'

'Right.'

'Well, I'll fill you in on that after you bring me up to date on Sisk.'

'I'll be interviewing her in the interrogation room in a few minutes. You can't be in there, but you can hear and see through a two-way mirror, if you'd like. You can't use anything either of us says in the paper unless you clear it with me,

108

though. Now what have you turned up that's one, so important, and two, so hilarious that you hung up on me?'

But they were interrupted by a message that Miss Sisk was waiting in the interrogation room. Duffy positioned Jennifer where she could see and hear best, then told her to be ready for anything.

'What do you mean by that?'

'I'm gonna push her pretty hard. For one thing, she could be guilty.'

'For sure, or is she just the one you're concentrating all your efforts on right now?'

He smiled at her. 'Both.'

He pulled back a curtain that allowed Jennifer to see clearly into the interrogation room where a matron sat in the corner and Josie Sisk sat on one side of a wooden table, smoking idly, but tapping one foot on the floor.

Duffy appeared distracted as he entered the room and didn't look Josie in the eye at first. 'Hi, Miss Sisk,' he said quickly.

'Ms.,' she corrected.

'Hi, *Miss* Sisk,' he repeated with emphasis, surprising both Jennifer and the matron and causing Josie to widen her eyes, narrow her mouth, look up and around the room, and nod knowingly, as if she had just fully realized what she had got herself into.

'My name is Duffy — '

'I know who you are.'

' — and this is Matron Gladys Sprague.'

'I know who she is too.'

'Well, good. Since you know who everyone is,

I want to tell you that we appreciate your turning yourself in and saving us a lot of time, trouble, and expense trying to track you down.'

'Don't mention it.'

'You have the right to remain silent, Miss Sisk, and I suggest you exercise it.' It was the first time Duffy had looked her in the eye. 'Anything you say can and will be used against you in a court of law.'

'I know my rights. I been busted before. Anyways, how come you're collarin' me when I came in on my own?'

'You have the right to have a lawyer present with you while you are being questioned. If you can't afford one, a lawyer will be appointed for you. Do you understand these rights as I have explained them to you?'

'Yeah, yeah.'

'Do you waive the right to a lawyer?'

'I can afford judges — what do I need a lawyer for?'

'Then you're waiving the right to have an attorney present?'

'Yeah!'

'And you're obviously waiving your right to silence.'

'Yeah.'

'Do you understand that you are being placed under arrest for the murders of Robert Block and Adrienne Eden?'

'Both of 'em?'

'That's correct. Did you murder only one of them?'

'No! I didn't murder nobody! I just didn't know I was gettin' busted for both of 'em.'

'Which murder did you think you were under suspicion for?'

'Adrienne.'

'Why?'

'Because I was there at her place that day.'

'You weren't at Block's before he was killed?'

'Plenty of times. I was s'posed to have breakfast with him that morning. Or at least breakfast at his place. He wasn't eatin'.'

'Why not?'

'Who knows? He gave up eatin' a couple of months ago.'

'Why didn't you show up?'

'For breakfast?'

'Uh-huh.'

'He called and tol' me Adrienne was coming over.'

'What time was this?'

'About seven-thirty I guess, quarter to eight.'

'When were you supposed to have been there?'

'About eight-thirty.'

'Why couldn't you be there if Adrienne was there?'

'What are you, crazy or somethin'? Adrienne didn't know about Bobby and me.'

'Can I ask you a personal question, Miss Sisk?'

'You already have. Lots of 'em.'

'I want to ask one more, and I don't mean to offend you.'

'You're trying to get me on two murders I didn't do, and you don't want to offend me?'

'Miss Sisk, how did you get next to two reasonably intelligent men when you sound so stupid?'

She glared at him. 'What're you sayin'?'

'I'm saying I don't understand how a newspaperman — a graduate of Medill School of Journalism — and another journalism student at the same respected university could see anything in an uneducated type like you. Nothing personal.'

It was all Jennifer could do to keep from bursting into laughter, though she was shocked at Duffy's approach, as was the matron whose eyes seemed to be popping out of her head.

'You don't know where I been educated, pal. I graduated from Senn High School and then I went away to college.'

'You went *away* to college?' Duffy said, pulling his note pad from his pocket and quickly leafing to the right page. 'You call flunking out of the nursing training after four weeks at Harper Community College in Palatine because of reading deficiency *going away* to college?'

'I had to live with a girlfriend in the suburbs for a while.'

'You apparently aren't going to answer my question.'

'About Ed and Bobby? Sure, I'll answer it. They never hit me as bein' so bright. What's so special about writin' for a newspaper or bein' in the college team? Why do they like me? I'm a fun girl — what can I tell ya?'

'You lied to me about Adrienne not knowing about you.'

'Well, she knew about me. She knew me, you know? But she didn't know I was seein' Bobby.'

'Were you aware that she had a key to his apartment?'

'I never thought about it much, but it doesn't surprise me. They were engaged.'

'You didn't worry about being caught in there with him?'

'There's a chain lock. Nobody's gettin' in there while we're in there unless we let 'em.'

'Where were you going to go if Adrienne showed up?'

'I don't know. I never thought about it. Never happened.' She chuckled. 'Luckily.'

'How did Bobby Block die?' Duffy asked.

'TV news says somebody poisoned him. Only I don't know what they put it in, 'cause like I say, he wasn't eatin', far as I could tell. Maybe they put it in his water.'

'What were you doing in his apartment the night before?'

'What are you talkin' about?'

'You were there. Several witnesses saw you come and go.'

'I'm not sayin' I wasn't there. I'm just wonderin' if you really don't know.'

'In other words, it was just a social call.'

'Right, exactly. Social. I mean, let's face it, Bobby and I weren't a couple. We didn't go out, you know what I mean? Adrienne got around, had a lot of friends. Anyway, I'm going with Ed, and just because he doesn't mind me seein' Bobby now and then, when I go out, I go out with Ed.'

'Uh-huh, and you really think Adrienne didn't know about you and Bobby?'

'I don't think so.'

'What were you doing at Adrienne's the day she died?'

'I was going to threaten her.'

Now even Duffy was shocked. 'You were?'

'Yes, I was.'

'Why?'

'Because I heard she was flirting with Ed.'

'Adrienne was flirting with Ed?'

'That's right.'

'And that's not good?'

She swore. 'You're right.'

'You can see Bobby on the side, even though he's engaged to Adrienne, but if Adrienne makes a move on your man, you're going to threaten her?'

'That's right.'

'How does that compute?'

'How what?'

'How does that figure? Make that make sense for me — that it's OK for you to fool around with her guy, but it's not all right for her to make eyes at yours.'

'I never said what I was doing was OK. But Ed didn't mind, and Adrienne didn't know, so I kept doin' it. If Ed didn't like it, he coulda tol' me. And if Adrienne found out, she shoulda put up a fuss, just like I was going to. If a woman don't fight for her man, she don't deserve to keep him.'

'Uh-huh. So what were you going to do to Adrienne?'

'Just scare her a little. Hurt her if necessary.'

'You're serious?'

'You heard me. I had a weapon. I'd have used it. I'd have killed her if she'd given me a reason.'

'You amaze me, Josie.'

'Yeah, why's that?'

'You're under arrest for murder, and I assume you want to talk your way out of it.'

'Yeah.'

'You're not doing a very good job.'

'Well, I'm just tellin' the truth. I knew you had me at both places before Bobby and Adrienne were found, so I decided honesty was the best policy.'

'That doesn't fit you.'

'Honesty doesn't?'

'No.'

'You heard me lie yet today?'

'You stretched it a little on going away to college.'

'I did? I didn't mean to. Palatine may not seem far to you, buddy, but leavin' the city is a trip for me.'

'So you went to Adrienne's to scare her and maybe even hurt her. What was your weapon?'

'A .22.'

'Pistol?'

'Yeah.'

'Ever use it before?'

'Nope.'

'Would you have used it?'

'You bet.'

'What would have made you use it?'

'If she gave me any grief.'

'And did she?'

'Are you kidding? She answered my knock

115

and dropped dead right there. I just shut the door and ran, man.'

'How did you know she was dead?'

'I felt for a pulse at her neck. Nothing. Dead — and I mean right away. Didn't that medical guy say Bobby was dead before he hit the floor too?' Duffy nodded. 'Must have been the same way here. I thought about Bobby and knew the same person prob'ly pulled both jobs. I didn't want any of it. But on the way out I saw a lot of people coming in, and I had to try to look like I hadn't just seen somebody drop dead right in front of me. Did a pretty good job hiding it too.'

'Hiding it.'

'The fact that I had just seen that. I think I looked pretty normal.'

'Yeah, for someone driving a canary Porsche.'

'Yeah, only it's yellow.'

'Uh-huh.'

Duffy stood and stretched. Josie lit another cigarette. 'Something's still sticking in my craw,' he said finally. She looked up. 'It didn't bother you that this woman was still grieving the loss of her fiancé?'

'Oh, sure, that's what made me feel so bad later. Ed finally told me I shoulda gone to him before running over to her place, because whoever told me that she was seeing Ed didn't know the whole story. I asked him what *was* the whole story, and he said she was just cryin' on his shoulder. I believe him now.'

'Who told you about Adrienne seeing Ed?'

'A guy at the *Tribune*. Chris.'

'Really? Does Ed know that?'

'No, and he ain't gonna know either. He likes Chris.'

'Does Chris like him?'

'I know what you're driving at, but it's not true.'

'You know for sure?'

'I do. It's something Chris likes people to think about him, but it's definitely not true. Thing is, I knew Chris long before I met Ed or Bobby.'

'Wonderful.'

'So what happens to me now? Can I go?'

'I'm afraid not.'

'You don't believe me? You think I murdered these two people?'

'Actually I don't, but you were at both scenes. You had a motive in at least one case. I don't know if you studied enough nursing at Harper to work out how to poison someone. But if I didn't detain you until we could clear you, I'd be delinquent in my duty.'

'I was a juvenile delinquent once.'

'You'd better get a lawyer, Josie.'

'OK.'

12

Cap Duffy roared when he heard the Chris Young story. Then he asked Jennifer what she thought of his interview with Josie Sisk.

'You were pretty tough with her, Cap. But I'll tell you this — I think she's innocent. I don't think she's got the brains to pull off a sophisticated poisoning.'

'Unless she's dumb like a fox and a great actress. She was consistent anyway, wasn't she? I mean, we're talking about a girl with no light at the top of the stairs.'

'Any more on the poison?'

'Yeah, I got a call from Jake just after I got back to the office this morning. First he gave me an evaluation of some of the medicines and stuff we found in Block's apartment. Mostly vitamins and minerals, but lots of 'em, which Block would have had to have taken if he was really on a starvation-type diet. And protein powder, just like the kind you can get from these home-based mail-order businesses.

'Jake said he sent some tissue sample to the Centre for Disease Control in Atlanta. Their preliminary finding is that Block, at least, died of dioxin poisoning. They found one hundred parts per billion dioxin in his body fluid. One part per billion is considered hazardous to human health and has been known to cause cancer, liver damage, and birth defects.

'Jake says it's one of the most toxic substances known, and that with as dense a concentration as was found in Block's tissue, the man didn't have a chance.'

'Could it have caused Block's cancer?'

'Oh, no, this would not have been in his system long before it killed him.'

'How does that fit in with your theory — and Jake's — that it worked on a delayed release basis?'

'Good girl, Jenn. That's just the question the professional detective asked. Jake says they also found traces of some sort of a buffer, an agent that protects the system from the harmful effects of the poison for a brief period, not longer than twenty-four hours. And once that buffer has been eaten away or is absorbed into the system, the dioxin is left to its devices. Almost instantaneous death at that one hundred per billion concentration. They're sending a sample from Adrienne's body down there too.'

'It'll show the same, won't it?'

'Probably.'

'What do you make of their starvation diets? Were they setting themselves up for this? Is it still possibly a double suicide?'

'It's possible, but I can't make out the delayed effect part of it. If you're going to kill yourself, particularly in a double death pact, why not do it quickly and together? Who wants to inject himself and then wonder when it's going to happen?'

'Maybe he did it, and she knew how he did it, so she followed suit.'

'Maybe,' Duffy said. 'But it isn't a normal double suicide modus operandi.'

'It's not a normal *murder* modus operandi, Cap.'

'True enough. That's another reason I doubt the suicide idea, even though I thought of it first. Where does a guy get access to dioxin? Jake says the only place he knows of is at one of the disease control centres, and you'd have to be a doctor or a scientist to even study it. You'd have to be a criminal to remove it from the laboratory.'

'Where do they get dioxin, Cap?'

'Researchers bring samples of contaminated floodwater in for analysis. When dioxin is found, people are evacuated from their homes, the substance becomes quarantine in the lab, and the local or state Department of Health moves in to treat the area.'

Duffy agreed that Block's notebooks were the key to the success of the rest of the investigation, particularly when he got a glimpse of how detailed they were. 'If Sisk is innocent, as I fear, we're probably looking for someone we haven't considered yet,' he said.

'That's going to be the point of my first couple of columns about this case,' Jennifer told him.

'Futility?'

'You bet. Dead ends. Long hours. Frustration. It's like running in a maze. You see an opening, you charge through, you hit a wall, you go back, you start over again. You enjoy this?'

'I enjoy knowing that a break will come that will make everything make sense. When it starts to fall into place, it'll all happen at once, and we'll be saying, "Ah ha! That's why this and that's why that." '

'I hope so.'

'We have to stay optimistic, Jennifer. If you don't believe a break is coming, it's hard to stay in the game.'

'Tell me one thing. Is this a typical investigation?'

'I'll say this: It's not a typical way to die, but it's a very typical investigation. It's like a crossword puzzle. If this word is right, these will be right; but if that word is wrong, we start from scratch. We're starting from scratch, in effect, now, but at least we've got a lot of the undergrowth cleared away. We can start to get to the heart of the matter. We can say, who really did this if it wasn't all the people who could have or should have?'

'I think you just mixed a few metaphors there,' Jennifer said, 'but I see what you mean.'

'Tell me what a metaphor is, and I'll try to unmix them for you.'

'Forget it, Cap. That's my job. Listen, you're not sure about Sisk yet. How will you determine whether or not she's telling the truth?'

'About all I can do is assign some people to check out her background with a fine-tooth comb to see if there's a link to dioxin or someone with access to dioxin there anywhere. See, the poison that killed Block — and most likely Eden too — is the smoking pistol. Whoever's got the dioxin source has the means. None of the people we've investigated so far had more than motive and opportunity, and that's not enough. When the means is as bizarre as it is in this case, if we can find someone with the means, we may not have to work so hard to establish the motive and opportunity.'

'Interesting,' Jennifer said.

'Exhausting.'

'I hear you.'

Duffy paged carefully through the first Block notebook, which covered almost the first two weeks of January. 'I can't make heads or tails of it,' he admitted. 'I can make out the dates and times, but little else. Can you read it, Jennifer?'

'I can read it, but it doesn't mean much to me either. See, here in mid-February of the fourth notebook I recognize his notes from a Police Department press conference we both attended.'

'What's it say?' Duffy said. 'Anything interesting?'

'Nah. It was just that thing about the police pension fund and benefit committee.'

'Not interesting, all right. I had hoped these notebooks would reveal something good.'

'You want me to just read through them aloud? You can make notes of anything you think is worth checking on.'

'I guess so.'

For sounding so unenthusiastic about the exercise, Duffy took a ton of notes. Every time Jennifer read off a set of initials or tried to guess the meaning of an abbreviation, he jotted it down. Often he looked over her shoulder to help her make out a particularly scribbly entry. Their break came early that evening when she read a note entered 9:00 a.m., Monday, February 28.

It appeared like this:

> Recd. perm. fr. PT on exp. Can use A if kp
> hm pstd. Phd. BC off. for appt. Thu. 10.3 a.
> K. Av.

Jennifer interpreted it this way, laboriously, for Cap:

'Received permission for, or maybe from — and I assume PT is someone's initials, yeah, the, uh, managing editor at the *Trib* is Phil Thornton. That a safe assumption then?'

'If you're sure that's his name — yeah, let's run with it.'

'OK, then he received permission from Thornton on e-x-p. Hm. E-x-p.'

'Explanation?' Duffy said.

'I don't think so. It's something he needs the boss's permission for.'

'Experience?'

'Maybe. Permission for experience doing what? Something undercover maybe? Maybe it's an exposé on something or someone.'

'E-x-p short for exposé?'

'Yeah!' Jennifer said. 'I just said that, didn't I? OK, he received permission from Thornton for an exposé, but on what? Can use A if he keeps him posted. I don't know who A is, maybe someone else on the staff, but he can use A, I'm guessing, if he keeps Thornton posted. Why would he have to keep Thornton posted if he used someone else on staff? Maybe it's someone not on staff. Adrienne!'

'You're assuming a lot,' Duffy said, 'but keep going. He can use Adrienne in the exposé?'

'I think so. Then he phoned BC office. BC is obviously someone's initials. And got an appointment for Thursday at ten-thirty in the morning. K Avenue — oh boy, that could be anything.'

Duffy furrowed his brow. 'If I had the manpower, I'd call every place of business with the initials BC on every street in Chicago starting with a K and find out which one of 'em had an appointment with Block on — what would it be? Thursday, March third at ten-thirty in the morning.'

'But Cap, you're assuming too much. We don't know if BC is a person's name or a company name. We don't know if the Thursday was the immediately following one. We don't know if Block used his own name in making the appointment, but I would highly doubt it. All BC would have to do, whoever that is, is see Bobby's name in the paper as a police reporter, and if the exposé is anything serious, Block is a dead man.'

'I agree I don't have enough yet to start the search, Jennifer, but do you realize what you just said? You said if BC, the company or the person, found out who Block was, he'd be a dead man. And he is a dead man. You keep studying the notes — my advice would be to jump to the following Thursday — while I call, what was the editor's name?'

'Phil Thornton.'

'Yeah, Thornton, to see if he knew any of the details.'

Jennifer found the entry for Thursday, March 3 and read:

> Init. int. unevent., BC not in. Set for diag.
> tsts., EKG, etc., Mon. No break. Mon. ur.
> samp.

At the bottom of the page, she read 'Ken. Ave.' and was eager to tell Duffy. He returned with bad news from Thornton.

'He really wants to help all he can, but he said he simply agreed in principle to Block's exposé — he makes it a practice not to involve himself, even to the point of not knowing the target. He just wants to know in advance in case legal questions arise. He was very curious to know where we got Block's notebooks. I told him we uncovered a lot of stuff in the course of the investigation.'

Jennifer made a face at him.

'You didn't want me to tell him you stole them

from Young who had stolen them from Block's desk, did you?' Duffy asked.

'No, but I didn't want to be responsible for your lying to him, either.'

'Did I lie to him?'

'By omission you did.'

'Same way you did when you didn't tell me you were seeing Young in the park?' Duffy said. Jennifer winced. 'You could have got yourself killed. He was a murder suspect, you know.'

'I know. I almost killed *him*, Cap.'

She showed him the entry she had been studying. 'If this is the address down here, that narrows it down some, doesn't it?' she said.

'Some. Kenmore? Kendale? Kendall? Kenwood? Should be able to find a BC on one of the Ken-something streets.'

'But his use of BC this time makes it look more like a person, doesn't it? And if he has to bring a urine sample and have diagnostic tests the following Monday, is he meeting with a doctor? Is BC a doctor? It wouldn't be the same doctor who's treating his cancer if it's tied in with this exposé.'

'If it *is* an exposé, Jennifer. We're still guessing.'

'C'mon, Cap, we're onto something and you know it. Where's the optimism?'

'I left it in bed last night.'

'Let's look at Monday the seventh of March.'

Gluc. tst. Foul. Boring wtng. Fml. Orntl.
Dr. elus, abt. educ., dbt. MD. BC not in.

Off. grl, says seldm. Inj. appt. supp. Prt.
lks. lk. commrcl. stf.

'Now I'll admit you may be onto something, Jennifer. Translate that mess for me.'

She studied it for several minutes. 'I think he's saying he had a glucose test he didn't like, probably where they make you drink that concentrated Coke-type stuff. He waited a long time, like you do with those crazy tests, and he was bored. The next part I don't know. Is he saying there's a female doctor who's elusive about her education? He's doubting her M.D. degree?'

'What's "Orntl."?'

'I couldn't tell you, Cap. Ornithologist?'

'Ha!' he said. 'Now I've got one on the brilliant columnist! He's going to a bird doctor?'

Jennifer smiled. 'Chalk one up for Broderick Crawford. Twenty-one-fifty to headquarters.'

'Headquarters by,' he said. 'Only a true "Highway Patrol" devotee could appreciate *that*.'

'You're talking to one,' she said, extending her hand.

He shook it. 'The originals?'

'Of course not,' she said. 'You've got me by ten years. Reruns only.'

'I'm sure,' he said, turning back to the notebooks. 'I can see we're going to need Jake's input on this.'

13

Dr. Jacob Steinmetz arrived with a large brown paper bag filled with take-away Chinese food. Trying to suppress a grin, he growled about having to work on a Saturday night, but it was apparent to Jennifer that he secretly enjoyed playing detective.

'Jennifer thinks she's onto something here, Jake,' Duffy said, 'and it's obvious to us we're heading in a medical direction.'

Jennifer flipped back to the Monday, March 7, entry as they sampled Jake's gifts. 'I love Oriental food,' she said.

'Oriental!' Cap said. 'Maybe that's what "Orntl." stands for!'

'Lemme see that,' Jake said. 'Wow, you guys are reaching. It could mean Oriental, I guess, but what does that tell you?'

Duffy took over. 'That he had a foul, boring

glucose test and that there was a female, Oriental doctor who was elusive when he asked about her education, so he doubted her medical degree.'

Jake almost doubled over in laughter. 'It sounds like a Peter Sellers movie! What else is there?'

Duffy was not amused. 'If you see any other possibilities, Jake, we're open. We've been staring at this scribbling long enough.'

With his mouth full, Jake waved an apology and bent over the notebook. Jennifer continued, 'BC not in. I'm guessing now that that's the doctor he wants to see. Office girl says seldom?'

'That would fit,' Jake agreed with a twinkle. 'If he's the main doctor, he would seldom be in, right?'

'But what kind of a doctor is he?' Duffy said. 'He gives glucose tests, EKGs, and all that.'

'I don't know, Cap. There can be a lot of reasons for both those tests. What else can you make out here?'

'I haven't been able to make anything out of the next few lines,' Jennifer admitted. 'He's making some kind of a point here. What do you think?'

The three of them sat on the edges of their chairs and hunched over the little notebook, staring at the entry:

Inj. appt. supp. Prt. lks. lk. commrcl. stf.

Jake tried, 'Injection appointment support. That makes no sense, and I don't know what p-r-t is.'

'The capital P means a new sentence,' Jennifer said, 'so the first three words stand alone. I don't know what p-r-t is either, but the rest of that last line is "looks like commercial", um, maybe "staff" or "stuff".'

Steinmetz suddenly stood and bent from the waist, raising his glasses to his forehead and pushing his face a few inches from the page, blocking Duffy's and Jennifer's view. 'May I?' he said, picking up the notebook and carrying it near an overhead light.

'By all means,' Duffy said. 'What is it, Jake? What've you got?'

'If p-r-t means "protein", he's saying it looks like the commercial stuff, which is just what the lab thought of the stuff they found in his kitchen cupboards! BC could stand for bariatric clinic where they give these glucose tests and EKGs before starting people on these liquid protein diets!'

'Are they legit?' Jennifer asked. 'Why would he expose them?'

'If they're prescribing stuff that they then supply, and it's commercial protein powder, then they're breaking the law. And of course, if the doctor's staffing his office with nonmedical personnel, they're probably counselling, diagnosing, and administering tests that only an M.D. is licensed to do.'

Jake turned back to the page, then sat heavily as if it had all just hit him like a ton of bricks. 'If i-n-j means injection, then a-p-p-t s-u-p-p could mean appetite suppressant, of which we found traces in both bodies! It *is* a bariatric clinic!'

'But why would he say BC is not in, if he was referring to a bariatric clinic?' Jennifer asked.

'Yeah,' Duffy said, 'and do you know of any bariatric clinics on a street like Kenmore, or Kendale, or Kendall, or Kenwood, or something like that?'

Steinmetz squinted in thought. 'The only doctor I can think of on a K Street is Duke Creighton on Kendall. He's been known to follow the trends, put people on severe diets, that type of thing. Used to be quite the playboy too, owns a yacht and all the rest, but he's getting on now. Must be close to retirement.'

'Duke his real name?' Duffy asked, pulling a fat phone book off the top of a filing cabinet.

'Seems maybe not,' Jake said, 'but I don't think I know his real name.'

Duffy leafed through the phone book, stopped in the Bs, ran his finger down the page and peered intently at the entry for Creighton on Kendall. He straightened up and twirled the book around on the table so it was right side up for Jennifer and Dr. Steinmetz.

They bent close to read: 'Brewster (Duke) Creighton, general practice, specializing in nutrition and bariatrics.'

'OK,' Jake said, 'let's just slow down a minute. Block may have been doing some kind of a series on Creighton, and it may have been an exposé. He may also have simply been on a doctor-supervised, liquid protein diet.'

'Jake, it's the first solid lead we've got. Let me ask you something. Is there a traditional location for appetite suppressant injections?'

'Not really. It's fairly common to administer them to the patient just below the hip, while the patient is standing. But Cap, Duke Creighton is a fine doctor. Always has been. Was some sort of a Chicago sports hero years ago, an Olympian or some such thing, maybe on a rowing team.'

'So we shouldn't check him out because he rowed a boat for the U.S. of A., Jake?'

'I'm not saying that. I just think you have to move cautiously when you start accusing a renowned doctor of running a clinic worthy of an exposé.'

'That's not all I'd accuse him of, Jake,' Duffy said. 'I think he worked out who Block was and added a little something to Bobby's last appetite suppressant.'

Jake looked stony, but he didn't argue.

'It'll all be in here if it's true,' Jennifer said, patting the stack of notebooks.

The three spent until 11:00 p.m. piecing together startling information from the scribbled cryptic notes of a dead man.

On March 14 Bobby had involved Adrienne in the scam under the name Betty Miller.

The entry for March 17 revealed he was using the name Daniel Edmonds.

March 23 revealed a note that indicated that the office girl, a Kirsten Moon, had offered to aid him in getting more than he was entitled to from Blue Cross/Blue Shield for his treatments. 'You pay $50, I put down that you paid $75, and they pay you 80 per cent of that, or $60.'

Block's notes indicated that he asked if she

wanted a cut. 'I wouldn't know what to do with more money,' she had replied.

'It still doesn't prove anything about the murders,' Jake said miserably, late in the evening. But his futile defence of an old acquaintance, one he admitted he had not seen for more than five years, was hollow and nearly unheard.

Block's research into the records of one of the leading home-based mail-order businesses in the country revealed that Dr. Brewster Creighton was its leading seller of protein powder and had won innumerable trips and other prizes.

'I can't believe Duke would do that,' Jake lamented. 'It's against the law to prescribe the stuff, and no doubt it's against the buying service rules too.'

Jennifer interpreted a March 30 entry this way:

> My own doctor says the weight loss is OK
> and the protein and vitamins are not
> harmful, though the big C is acting up
> again. I'll look trim in the coffin.

'You gotta admit that's ironic,' Duffy said, shaking his head.

'Big C means colon or cancer?' Jennifer wondered.

'Either one,' Jake said. 'What's the difference?'

The April 1 notes showed Block's confidence that his cover was still intact.

> I never want my picture in the paper like
> my former boss. Her undercover days are
> over.

April 8, Block noted that he had told Phil Thornton that he would be ready with the first instalment of the big exposé by the last week of April for the Sunday, May 1 *Tribune*.

> I asked if he wanted to know what it was all about. He said no, but if it was big enough he could try to get it in the *Tribune Magazine*. I said no, because once it broke, it would have to run every day for at least a week. He asked if my weight loss had anything to do with it. I lied and said no. He'll find out soon enough.

April 19, Block wrote that he was looking forward to the appetite supressant injection the next day.

> They start to wear off now after about five days. It's all I can do to hang on until Wednesday afternoons. Cheated only twice. No noticeable difference in weight loss pattern. Medical records show no listing for Filipino female "doctor" who handles most of the work. Still have never seen BC. On his boat somewhere KM says.

Several records indicated a discrepancy in charges and mode of payment, depending on which of the staff waited on Block and/or Adrienne. Her weight loss was slower and less dramatic, but she cheated more.

The next entry, under the same date, made Jennifer tearful.

> Wrote to Jenn. Fence-mending long
> overdue. Guess I'll just tell her straight
> out. No excuse, but a reason. Hope she
> agrees to see me. Wouldn't blame her if
> not.

She only hoped he had got her message to phone back.

'I've got enough to get a warrant right now,' Duffy said.

'You may be able to get a coroner on a Saturday night,' Jake said. 'But I'd like to see you rouse a judge. Anyway, you don't know where to begin to look for Creighton.'

'I don't want Creighton yet. I just want access to his office tomorrow. Nobody will be there on a Sunday. If I can get clearance for you, Jake, will you join me? I'm gonna need help deciphering medical notes and records.'

'I guess so,' Steinmetz said. 'But this is going down hard.'

'I can imagine,' Duffy said. 'How long have you known Creighton?'

'A couple of decades at least. I met him when we were both on an emergency public safety board for the Fox Lake River flood project.'

Jennifer and Duffy stared at him. He looked from one to the other before realizing what he had said. Creighton was the type of doctor who would have access to disease germ samples and poisons. Jake buried his head in his hands.

'OK if I go now?' he asked finally.

'Sure, Jake. And thanks a lot. Can I call you tomorrow if I get the warrant?'

Jake nodded.

'And you won't tell a soul what we uncovered here tonight until we make an arrest, huh?'

He nodded again and pulled on his coat as he shuffled wearily out the door.

'I'm sorry to be calling so late, Mrs. Cole. This is Detective Cap Duffy of the Chicago Police Department calling for the Judge.... Thank you, ma'am.

'Judge, I'm terribly sorry to wake you, and you know I wouldn't if it weren't important.... Yes sir, we met once in the late sixties during an Illinois Bureau of Investigation drug bust in the western suburbs when you were with the State's attorney's office, and we met again during the Tylenol murder investigations...in Mr. Fahner's office, yes sir.

'Well, it's this double poisoning murder of the newspaperman, Block, and his fiancée, Adrienne Eden.... Yes, sir, if I can get a warrant to search a doctor's office tomorrow, I feel confident we'll be able to make an arrest.... A messenger? No, sir, if you did that, I'd come myself to pick it up tonight.... Thank you, sir. I appreciate that. Here's the doctor's name and address.'

The judge also recognized Creighton's name and asked several questions about the investigation before issuing a warrant that Duffy himself drove over to pick up.

When Duffy returned at about midnight, Jennifer had more information for him. 'Look at this entry for April 15. It looks like he's saying, "Told Mac about BC. Probably shouldn't have, but he'll keep it. A's appetite suppressant wore off early last week too. She had another yesterday morning.'' So, Cap, Bobby has his next shot the following Wednesday afternoon and dies Thursday morning. She has hers that same Thursday morning, a week after this entry, and dies the next afternoon.

'You realize what that means, Cap? She had her injection and had that poison in her system by the time she showed up at his apartment just after noon on the day he died.'

Cap still had his hat on, and now he pushed it back on his head and folded his arms. 'What we have to determine tomorrow is how Creighton got onto Block and Eden and who gave the lethal injections. If one of these office girls did it, which is unlikely, whether Creighton himself actually prepared the shots, or whether he even administered them. Anything on that in Block's notebook?'

'No. The twelfth book ends April sixteenth. He died on the twenty-first.'

'Well, there should be a lot of corroboration in the doctor's office, unless he was smarter or more careful than we thought. I'm gonna grab some shut-eye and then visit that office first thing in the morning. You?'

'I'm afraid I can't join you tomorrow, Cap.'

'*What?* We're getting to the best part, lady!'

'I know, but I go to church on Sundays, and I try to work as little as possible.'

He smiled at her. 'Where do you go to church?'

'These days up in Waukegan at Jim's church.'

'How about a deal?'

'A deal?'

'Yeah. My wife and I will join you for church, then you two join Jake and me at the doctor's office.'

'Jim would love that.'

'Yeah. My wife doesn't like that snooping around sort of stuff, so I'd drop her off at home maybe after dinner and before we head to Creighton's office.'

'You're not worried about losing time on this?'

'Nah. The only other people who know about it are Jake and the judge, and they won't be telling anyone. I'll be hard pressed to get any help rounding up Creighton on a Sunday anyway. My plan is to get everything we need at his office and try to collar him Monday. We got a deal?'

'Sure, Cap. Are you sure you want to?'

'If your church is like the one I went to when I was nine, where they still believe, how did you say it — ?'

'That there's a God who loves you and a Jesus who saved you from your sins?'

'Yeah. Then I'd like to check it out. It'll be a little late notice for Maryann, but she's always game.'

14 Cap and Maryann Duffy were so impressed with Jim's church that they asked if they could come back the following week.

'You could even come tonight,' Jim said at lunch.

'That would be even better,' Maryann said, surprising everyone, including herself. 'I mean, it's just that everyone seemed so happy and at ease and — well, enthusiastic.'

'We are,' Jennifer said.

'What impressed me,' Cap said, 'was how obvious it was that everyone just *believes*. I mean, they talk about it, sing about it, pray about it, smile about it.'

'Not *it*,' Jim said, smiling.

'Yeah,' Cap said, slightly embarrassed. 'I know.' He pointed up.

'I was almost going to join you on your little

escapade this afternoon,' Maryann said, 'just so maybe we could talk a little more about it. But if we're going tonight, I won't have to.'

'I don't know how you can refuse the invitation,' Jennifer said.

'Believe me, it's easy,' she said. 'I know it's important, and I'm proud that Harold is good at it. But it always gives me the willies to be poking around in other people's things.'

'But we have a warrant, Darling,' Cap said.

'I know, and if that makes you comfortable, enjoy yourselves. I'll pass.'

'But you *will* come tonight?' Jennifer asked.

'I wouldn't miss it,' she said. 'I confess it was not at all what I expected. I was really afraid at first and almost didn't come. But Harold told me about the good times he'd had in church as a child, so I thought it was worth a try. It left me with a million questions, I'll tell you that.'

'Well,' Jim said, 'we don't have all the answers, but you can try us, and we can at least point you to someone who could be more helpful.'

Dr. Jacob Steinmetz was waiting in his car across the street from Brewster Creighton's office when Cap Duffy pulled up with Jim and Jennifer.

Cap stopped next to Jake's car, and it was immediately obvious that the coroner was in a bad mood. 'Let's park a couple of blocks down and not appear so obvious,' Cap suggested. 'I've tipped off the burglar alarm company and the local precinct station in case we can't get past the wiring, but Jim has the tools we need.'

'Duke is in town,' Jake said.

'How do you know that?' Cap asked.

'I couldn't help myself, Cap. I drove past his place. His camper is parked at the side, and the boat's in the garage. I saw him in the garden this morning.'

It was all Duffy could do to keep from exploding. 'Did he see you, Jake? If you blew this thing for us, he could have already been in there destroying all the evidence and — '

'I didn't say anything to him, Cap. He didn't see me. But I almost wish I had tipped him off.'

'What if he's guilty?' Cap asked.

'That's the only thing that kept me from it. That, and the fact that you made me promise last night. I'm a man of my word, Cap. But breaking into a doctor's office goes against everything I've ever believed in.'

'So does murder, doesn't it, Doctor?'

Jake stared at him. Cap pointed down the street, and Jake followed him. When the cars were situated, Jake joined the other three in Cap's car. 'Jim will go first,' Cap said, 'and try to get in without tripping the alarm. Once he's in, we follow nonchalantly, as if the office is open and we're expected.'

'You don't see any value at all in allowing Duke to come down here and let you in so you don't have to break into his files and everything?' Jake tried.

'Doc, I gotta tell ya, that's a little naïve. He'll call a lawyer to get a temporary restraining order on the warrant, and that will give him all the time he needs to destroy anything that would prove his guilt.'

'Or innocence,' Jake said.

'If there's nothing in the office that implicates him, then maybe he *is* innocent. We're not gonna plant anything, Jake. I'm going in there with you and one of the straightest cops I've ever worked with. Jim is Officer Friendly, for pete's sake, and Jennifer would never let me get away with anything underhanded, which I wouldn't try anyway. You can be of great help to me today, Jake, if you're not just in there trying to defend your buddy.'

'He's not my buddy,' Jake said, 'but he's a brother in the profession.'

'He also took the Hippocratic oath, right?' Cap said.

Jake nodded.

'And if he violated that, you want to see him answer for it just as much as I do, maybe more.'

Cap took Jake's lack of response as consent and nodded to Jim, who left the car and walked briskly a block and a half to the Creighton Medical Building. Jim tried the front door, then moved around to the back where he slipped a thin strip of metal between the door and its frame, slicing the wire to the burglar alarm. That took care of the remote feed to the police station, but opening the door would trip the local siren on the building.

Jim used a bent wire pick to trip the lock almost as quickly as a key would have done the job, then placed one hand on the glass next to the door and the other hand on the handle. He spotted the wire to the siren inside the building. He yanked open the door and heard the scream of the horn as he raced through the shallow lobby and swiped at the nearly hidden wire with his metal strip. The siren ceased.

Jim returned and relocked the back door, then made his way through to the front where he unlocked the door and pushed it open a few inches to signal the others to join him. When they were in, Jim locked the front door and moved cautiously toward Creighton's private office. He dropped to the floor and peered through the crack under the bottom of the closed door.

He motioned to Cap to join him in the front lobby again. 'There's a unit next to Creighton's desk that could be any medical device, but if it is, it's the only one in that office.'

'What are you saying? What do you think it is?'

'A sound-activated alarm.'

'Have no fear,' Duffy said with a grin, and he produced from his pocket a high frequency tone generator.

'You think of everything, don't you?' Jim asked.

'I'm an old thirty-nine,' Cap said. 'There's a reason for that. Would you like to do the honours?'

'Sure, what do I do?'

'Just aim it at the machine and give it one shot with this button. You won't hear a thing, but if we were outside, dogs would come running.'

Purcell edged back to the door and carefully laid the corner of the palm-sized device in the crack under the door. He pushed the button. 'How do I know if it worked?' he whispered.

'Like this,' Cap said, and he rapped loudly on the door. 'Gimme your pick.' And he popped the lock. The device had indeed been a sound detector, and if it had been on, it was now off.

'Did I do that?' Purcell asked.

'We'll never know,' Cap said. 'But who cares? We now own this place.'

After a quick tour to get the lay of the land, Duffy pulled everyone back into Creighton's private office. 'It's possible that people in the neighbourhood are already suspicious. If they call the cops, a squad will come and then tell them that we're authorized to be here. If they call Creighton, we could have trouble when he shows up. If anyone notices him arrive, let me know so I can get some back up. Since he's unaware of this, he could shoot us and not suffer for it.

'Jennifer, I want you to dig through the files in the reception area. See what you can find on Bobby and Adrienne's aliases, Daniel Edmonds and Betty Miller. Jake, check the medicine storage cabinets. You know what you're looking for.'

'Dioxin,' he said.

Duffy nodded. 'I'll go through the doctor's office, and Jim will float around, opening anything you want opened, damaging as few locks as possible. Jake?'

'Yeah.'

'If you find anything significant, don't touch it, hear?'

Jake nodded.

'Work quickly, because if someone *does* tip off Creighton, he'd be here how fast, Jake?'

'Oh, forty minutes I guess.'

'All right, we meet back here in twenty-five minutes with whatever you've got.'

Jake found six vials of unidentified substances that were clearly labelled as dangerous poisons. Yet they were in the same cabinet as the appetite suppressant. He wondered whether the poisonings could have been a mistake and if other victims might turn up. Yet the poisons would have to be evaluated to see if they contained dioxin.

Jennifer found a raft of information on patients Edmonds and Miller from appointment times to payment receipts, from prescriptions to diagnostic test results. She found one report that seemingly indicated a cancer-related blood problem, along with a note that the information was classified and not to be discussed with the patient. Attached to this report was a handwritten note from Dr. Creighton stating that this 'problem shall in no way affect or be affected by the protein diet programme'.

But she also found strange financial documents. The K. M., who must have been Kirsten Moon, had indeed falsified many records to Blue Cross/Blue Shield, initiating overpayments to patients from that company.

The plum of Jennifer's search was a small stack of notes concerning Edmonds and Miller that began early in March. The first several were copies of notes to Dr. Creighton that Mr.

Edmonds was continually requesting an appointment with him. The doctor's replies recommended stalling as long as possible, promising that perhaps he would see Edmonds in May, if his schedule cleared.

Suddenly, on April 18 there was a note from another girl in the office to Miss Moon, informing her that the doctor had called from his Wisconsin cabin at the weekend to find out when certain patients were scheduled for appointments. The note added, 'Kirstie, please call Dr. C. at his cabin and tell him when the following six are scheduled.' Among the list were both Edmonds and Miller.

A general note went to the staff the afternoon of April 18, informing them that the doctor would be in Wednesday afternoon and Thursday morning and could then be reached at his home until Sunday afternoon at three when he would return to Wisconsin.

Duffy had found little until he searched the cabinets lining the walls of Creighton's office. He had been through correspondence files, a petty cash fund, prescription pads, and equipment chests. But in one corner of a locked door of a locked cabinet was a small cash box, also locked. When Jim popped it open for him, Duffy knew he'd hit pay dirt.

In the box he found just over $11,000 in cash and a small ledger book with a rubber band around it, noting various payments and deposits. Creighton had apparently kept a stash of $20,000 in the box. But a payment was noted for Thursday evening, April 21, for $8,950 'to retire E.M. car loan'.

Duffy made a fast phone call to an associate and asked him to check telephone and bank records on two people, one of whom was Dr. Brewster Creighton. When Jennifer told Cap what she'd found, Duffy asked his boss to stake out the streets around the Creighton residence to see if he indeed planned to leave at 3:00 p.m. It was two-thirty.

When everyone had gathered in Creighton's office, Duffy summarized. 'We can place Creighton himself here at the time of Block's and Eden's last injections. Whether he administered them or not, we don't know. He could have prepared them anyway, then this Kirsten Moon or someone else could have given the shots without being aware of the contents of the syringes.'

'We'll have to examine the vials,' Jake reminded him.

'Of course. The key is, what made Creighton call from Wisconsin last weekend and decide to come in when Block and Eden were scheduled for appointments? Obviously, someone tipped him off, but who was it and how did they get his number in Wisconsin?'

'Would it had to have been either Young, McDevitt, or Sisk?' Jennifer asked.

'Probably,' Duffy said. 'Sisk probably knew nothing about it. What motive would she have had for exposing the scam? Young may have had the notebooks before Block died, but I can't think of his motive either. He told you, Jennifer, that he

147

hadn't read them, but for some reason he thought they might be important. Does that add up?'

'Really it does,' Jennifer said. 'As a newspaper-man, he would know that there would be detailed information in there, even if he didn't read it.'

'When was that entry in Block's journal that said he had told someone about BC?'

Jennifer pulled out the notebooks. 'Friday, April fifteenth. Says he told Mac. What are you thinking, Cap? McDevitt?'

'Could be. Say McDevitt calls here to rat on Block because he can't stand sharing Josie with him. He wants to sell the doctor some informa-tion that would save his practice from a ruinous exposé. The doctor isn't in, and to protect him, the staff probably says they can't give out his number but that they will call the doctor and give him a message. McDevitt makes the message pro-vocative enough that Creighton indeed calls him back. Within a day or two, Creighton makes arrangements to be back in his office for the two appointments, and once the deeds are done, he settles with McDevitt.'

'But what do you make of the cash journal entry, Cap?' Purcell asked.

'A good way to launder the money,' Duffy said. 'It goes from Creighton to McDevitt in cash, McDevitt deposits it in his account, then writes a cheque for that amount to pay off his car loan. He's that much richer because he now has the money he would have spent over the next three or four years in high car payments, but he's not all of a sudden flashing bills around. I've got someone checking on his bank statement right now. They're also working on the phone calls between here and Creighton's Wisconsin cabin during the last week.'

The phone rang, and everyone looked to Duffy. 'All right,' he said, 'it could be my man, or it could be that someone has tipped off Creighton. Jennifer, you answer it, and if it's Creighton, make him think it's his answering service.'

She picked up the phone. 'Doctor's office.'

'Dr. Duffy, please.'

She smiled and handed Duffy the phone. 'Yeah, Frank.... Oh, no! No mistake? Thanks, and stay close. We may need you. I may have to bluff him pretty good, but we'll want to make the arrest today.'

Duffy hung up without another word and began scrambling to put the office back in shape. 'My guys are tailing Creighton. He and his wife have left the house in their camper, but it appears they're heading this way. Jake, you and Jennifer and I will make it look like we haven't been here while Jim finds us a place inside here to wait for him.'

15

It seemed to take longer to put the office back the way it was than it had to put it in disarray. And things were slowed when Jim returned by Duffy's deciding to let him reorganize Creighton's office while Cap was on the phone to his contacts, pushing for information before Creighton showed up.

Jim had located a first floor landing that overlooked the back lobby and much of the reception area where at least three of them could watch Dr. Creighton as he entered. Duffy, because of his size, would fit in a cabinet at one end of Creighton's office, and, blocked by a filing cabinet, he could leave the door open far enough to view most of the room.

Meanwhile, with Duffy on the phone, Jim straightening Creighton's office, Jennifer tidying up the reception area, and Jake on the lookout after having relocked the medicine cabinets, they awaited Brewster Creighton.

'I see a couple of cars near yours!' Jake said. Duffy quickly ended his call and jogged to the front door. He peered down the street through the tinted glass lobby and pulled a walkie-talkie from his belt.

'One-nineteen to one-sixteen.'

'One-sixteen,' came the static filled response.

'Bill, you don't want three unmarked squads that close together and that close to this building, do you?'

'Ten-four, Cap. Repositioning. Any guess where the mark will pull in?'

'Ten-four, sixteen. Vehicle size should force him into north car-park entrance. He's likely to enter the building from the back. What do we know about his current ten-twenty?'

'Stand by.'

In less than a minute, Duffy's associate came back on with Creighton's approximate location and said, 'E.T.A. fifteen-hundred-fifteen.'

'What's he saying?' Jake asked.

'Estimated time of arrival is three-fifteen,' Cap said. 'Everybody ready?'

'What'd you get on the phone and bank stuff, Cap?' Jim asked.

'Plenty.'

Dr. Steinmetz, Jim, and Jennifer stationed themselves on the first floor, overlooking the back door, the main corridor, and the reception area, while Duffy climbed into the cabinet in Creighton's office.

'Nineteen to sixteen.'

'Go ahead, Cap.'

'Let me know when you spot the vehicle. I'll go off the air but will click you twice if I need you.'

'How do we get in, sixteen?'

'Stand by,' Duffy said, then hollered, 'Jim?'

'Yeah!'

'You'd better unlock the front door — in case we need help.'

'What if he comes to the front door? If it's unlocked it'll tip him off.'

'He may already know we're in here, Jim. That may be why he's coming. Well, pick a door to leave unlocked so I can tell my backups.'

'I'll unlock the back, Cap.'

Duffy told his backup.

At seventeen minutes after three, Duffy's walkie-talkie crackled the message. 'Nineteen to sixteen, vehicle sighted. Entering north car-park. Parking at edge in back. Driver leaving vehicle. Heading toward back door.'

'I'm going off the air, sixteen!' Cap said, 'And we're switching your unlocked door. Then he yelled, 'Jim! Lock the back door fast and unlock the front. Hide where you can. This is it!'

Jim could see Brewster Creighton across the back parking area about thirty feet from the back door, walking slowly, head down. Jim put one foot on the railing and leaped to the ground floor, bending low as he hit to cushion the impact. He flew into the lobby and turned the knob on the back door, stealing a glance at Creighton before running back through the corridor. The doctor did not appear to have seen him.

Jim slid into the front lobby and unlocked the door, but as he turned to dash back upstairs, he heard Creighton inserting his key into the burglar alarm shutoff, then into the back door. Jim plastered himself against the wall in the lobby and held his breath.

Creighton moved purposefully through the main corridor carrying a black leather bag. The broad, only slightly hefty, grey-haired doctor wore white leather shoes, rust-coloured trousers, a white turtleneck sweater, and a pale yellow sports coat. He opened examining room doors on either side of the corridor, quickly scanned them, and shut the doors again. Occasionally he would drop something in his bag.

When he got to the reception area, he pulled two of his medical degree certificates from the wall, then rummaged in the bottom of the desk drawer and replaced them with old photographs. At the end of the corridor, he took down a photo of himself and the rest of the 1940 United States Olympic rowing team and replaced it with a photocopy of his university diploma.

He also retrieved a couple of photographs of his wife and family, one of his parents, and a gold inlaid letter opener. From a cupboard he took his golf clubs and shoes and a camel-hair sports coat. He then made a quick trip to his camper, chatted briefly with his wife as he dropped off the stuff, and returned to the building.

He surveyed the rest of the ground floor one more time, picking up a few keepsakes here and there and dropping them into his coat pockets.

From one of the medicine cabinets he removed the six vials Jake Steinmetz had identified as poisons. Just outside his office he inserted a special key into a mechanism above his door to turn off the sound-activated alarm, then unlocked his door. Inside he moved quickly to a cabinet at the other end of the office from where Duffy hid.

Dr. Creighton slid open a door and pulled an expensive leather briefcase from the shelf and placed it carefully on his desk. He opened it and emptied nearly $80 from his petty cash fund into it, replacing the box in his desk drawer. He pulled two folders from his filing cabinet — stepping within three feet of the motionless Detective Cap Duffy — paused only briefly to leaf through them, and deposited them in his briefcase as well.

Creighton looked around the room once more and retrieved a couple of personal knickknacks and keepsakes, packing them neatly in his case. He then unlocked the cabinet in the corner, unlocked the smaller door, unlocked the cash box, and left it open.

Creighton went to the phone, dialled a number he read from a tiny slip of paper, let it ring once, then hung up. He closed his briefcase, spun the combination locks, unplugged the sound alarm, and sat on the edge of the desk, looking at his watch.

Within seconds the phone rang once and fell silent. As if on cue, Creighton slid the briefcase off the desk, left his office without relocking the door, left the building without resetting the central alarm, and locked the back door. He strode to his vehicle and pulled away.

'He's gone!' Jim shouted from the front lobby.

'He get anything significant?' Duffy asked, turning on his radio and announcing that he was back on the air.

'He took the poison,' Jake called as they met in the corridor.

Duffy called his backup. 'Nineteen to sixteen. Bill, he set this place up for someone. Don't let him get too far. He's got evidence we need, and we can't let him dump it. Let him get out of sight of here and take him.'

'Is he armed, nineteen?'

'I doubt it, but be careful.' He turned to the others. 'Let's clear out so we can stake this place out. Someone is coming, probably after dark. Anyway, I need time to figure out why Creighton takes eighty bucks and leaves more than $11,000 unlocked.'

By early evening Maryann Duffy had been called to cancel her evening plans with her husband and Jim and Jennifer. Jake Steinmetz had received permission to go home. Jim had been stationed with one of the three back-up cars situated within view of the front of the building.

Jennifer was in the back seat of Duffy's squad car, now positioned on an east-west street a half block behind the medical building, with a clear view of the parking area and back door. Duffy sat behind the wheel, alternately watching and reading a report hastily scribbled by one of his men, telling of the telephone bank activity of Brewster

Creighton. Several of Creighton's phone calls from Wisconsin and his office had been to a pay phone on the Northwestern campus.

Duffy had also been filled in on the preliminary questioning of Dr. Brewster Creighton, who had refused to answer any questions until his lawyer arrived. The vials had been sent to the lab, and the results, showing concentrated dioxin content, came back at about the time Creighton's lawyer arrived.

Creighton apparently refused to tell even his lawyer what he had done in his office, other than pick up a few items. The lawyer had demanded that charges be filed or his client released, but the Homicide Division was stalling as long as possible, using Sunday as an excuse not to have all the documents and personnel they needed and knowing they'd have an easier time if they had Creighton's accomplice.

At approximately 11:30 p.m., after Jennifer had exhausted her 'what-if' questions and was beginning to wonder if they weren't on a wild goose chase — which, Duffy told her, was not only entirely possible, but probable, given the odds in such situations — Duffy was informed by radio that an old car had been parked about three and a half blocks from his location and that the driver was now walking in that direction.

Duffy and Jennifer peered out and soon saw a figure approaching from the north, occasionally illuminating a piece of paper in its hand with a penlight. Reaching the north edge of the car-park to the medical building, the figure stayed in the shadows near a row of hedges and then angled directly toward the back door.

Duffy left his car with Jennifer right behind him and sidled up to the hedgerow to watch the figure unlock the back door, apparently with a key. As the figure edged down the corridor, again illuminating the paper with a light, Duffy crept through the back door and deftly stayed about thirty feet behind, Jennifer still on his heels, her heart racing.

The figure located Creighton's office door and pushed it open, using the light constantly now. Duffy and Jennifer slipped off their shoes and stole down the carpeted corridor, stopping a few feet from the office.

From inside, they could hear the opening of the cabinet, the inner door, the box. Money was being stuffed in pockets. Duffy sneaked to the other side of the door where he could see in through the crack.

The figure reached inside a short coat and withdrew two thin pint bottles, which looked like whisky containers. These were splashed around the floor from the cabinet, past the desk, and to the door, where the figure now stood not four feet from where Duffy crouched, his hand on the snub-nosed .38 in his shoulder holster.

As the odour of petrol wafted into the corridor, the dark figure pocketed the penlight and produced a disposable cigarette lighter. Backing and reaching for the door behind it, the intruder carefully held it open, still gazing into the office, lighter poised.

Duffy moved up from behind and stuck the

barrel of his pistol into the back of the man's neck, just above the spine, reaching around to the chin with his left hand. 'Drop it or you're a dead man, Ed,' he said, as McDevitt jumped, then struggled. The tall student whimpered and pulled against the force of Duffy's strangle hold, and somehow ignited the lighter and flipped it into the room.

The force of the blast drove both men into the corridor, and Duffy's gun bounced near McDevitt. Ed grabbed it and handed it to the detective, swearing and screaming. 'Kill me, you liar! You said I'd be a dead man! Shoot me! Shoot me!'

Duffy holstered his weapon as flames from the office licked at the corridor. McDevitt lay in a heap on the floor, sobbing. 'I had to make Bobby pay!' he said. 'I had to make him pay!'

'You're *all* going to pay,' Duffy said, grabbing the big man by his collar and his belt and using his own lithe strength and balance to drag McDevitt toward the back. Jennifer held the door open as Duffy yanked McDevitt to his feet and sent him stumbling past the bushes and safely out of range of the roaring fire.

Backup cars slid into the car-park, and Cap's aide from the Chicago Avenue station jumped out and ran toward the back door, shouting for Duffy.

'Over here, Bill!' Cap called. 'We're all OK.'

As Ed McDevitt was handcuffed and led to a squad car, Cap squeezed Jennifer's shoulder. She was shaking. He winked at her. 'You and Jim up to a little coffee at my place later tonight? We owe it to Maryann, don't we?'

Jennifer could hardly speak. 'Ask him,' she said, as Jim came charging around the corner of the burning building. He threw his arms around her and held her tight, not thinking, or at least not caring, that it was the first time he had held her in front of anyone.

Relief lit his face as it sank in that Jennifer was safe.